# IN KENSINGTON GARDENS ONCE...

# IN KENSINGTON GARDENS ONCE...

## H.R.F. Keating

*Drawings by Gwen Mandley*

FLAMBARD

# ACKNOWLEDGEMENTS

Some of these stories first appeared in the following publications:
'Blood and Bone' in *Alfred Hitchcock Mystery Magazine*
'Incident at Millionaires' Row' in *2nd Culprit*
'Mr Idd' in *3rd Culprit*
'Mrs Craggs and the Late Prince Albert' in Crimes Cleaned Up
'Speke' in *Ellery Queen's Mystery Magazine*
'Towards What Fate?' in *Midwinter Mysteries 5*

Flambard Press wishes to thank Northern Arts for its financial support.

First published in the UK in 1997 by Flambard Press
4 Mitchell Avenue, Jesmond, Newcastle upon Tyne NE2 3LA

Typeset by Barbara Sumner
Cover design by Gwen Mandley
Cover processed by Mike Davis
Printed by Cromwell Press, Broughton Gifford, Melksham, Wiltshire

A CIP catalogue record for this book is available from the British Library.

ISBN 1 873226 23 3

# CONTENTS

# VICTORIAN VALUES

Seated day after day, year after year indeed, in Kensington Gardens, looking much as I was when in the year 1837, aged nineteen, I rode away from Westminster Abbey after my Coronation, with here on my head the new, lighter crown made for me then with the jewels from the Imperial Crown which both my uncles had worn, the sceptre held too in my upraised right hand, looking out endlessly at the Round Pond, dotted with toy yachts in summer, ice-bound in winter, lost in the darkness of the nights, sparkling under the sun in the days, one becomes prey to dreadful ennui.

So it should be a matter of no surprise that when there takes place within my view some little drama, a meeting of lovers, an altercation of some sort, even a small boy falling over and grazing his knee, I should take a particular, possibly ridiculous, interest in its every aspect.

As I did over the odd train of events that happened just yesterday. There is a wooden bench a few yards away to my right as I sit with my back to poor old Kensington Palace, scene in the days of Mamma's shunned, impoverished early widowhood of my very unhappy upbringing – that sprig of holly tied under my chin to teach me not to look downwards being the very least of it – in those dull, dark and dreadfully gloomy lower-floor rooms, haunt always of horrible black beetles.

I am just able, since my darling daughter, Loosy, contrived to sculpt us with our face turned a little to the right, to take note out of the corner of my eye of any persons sitting on the bench. Few do. Perhaps in our presence seated on our throne – year upon year, alas, decade after decade – they feel they should not loll at ease.

However, some time before noon yesterday a young woman came, dropped down on to it in the sunshine and began to read a volume she extracted from a sort of capacious leather reticule she carried. I took note of her, in much the way I was accustomed to observe whatever in my schoolroom days I chose to make the subject of my pencil. My gift of acute observation was commented upon on more than one occasion then.

The young woman appeared to be aged perhaps twenty-five, although I find with the ladies' fashions of the late twentieth century – if indeed the paucity of garments young people affect can be described as fashions – that it is not easy to fix upon precise ages. She wore no hat, as ladies seem not to have done for a number of years now, and I was able to see her abundant dark hair, not dressed in the manner I favoured at her age but nonetheless brushed smoothly to a fine gloss which, added to her other attractions, greatly became her. Before long I came to the conclusion that, despite the informality of her appearance, she was a person of the upper classes, or at least of the better section of the middle class. I had noticed, for example, as she passed in front of us, that she wore a wristwatch evidently of some considerable value, diamonds glinted in the setting, and her blue linen dress, though somewhat exiguous and without any of the ornament we ourself used to delight in, was plainly well made.

After a while, however, I saw that her eyes were no longer fixed on the page in front of her. I recalled indeed the difficulties I myself sometimes had in those gloomy rooms behind me with my lesson books – insufferable Latin – in happy contrast to the delight with which I devoured such few stories as were permitted to me.

I saw now that my young lady was glancing about her at the luncheon-hour crowds beginning to come into the Gardens. And before long I realised that her attention in particular was fixed upon a young man walking to and fro among the strollers on the broad path beside the Round Pond and on the Broad Walk immediately in front of ourself. Soon her book was altogether forgotten as she watched him. Every now and again I was able to see, too, a smile flit across her face.

It took me some time to decide what it was exactly in the way the young man was seemingly idly pacing about that caused this quick, little smile to appear. But eventually I realised that it came each time he turned and walked away with some rapidity from a person with whom he had appeared to be in close contact, though I never observed him engage anyone in conversation.

Eventually, watching the young man myself, in sympathy with the lady on the bench beside me, I came to realise what it was exactly he was doing.

To explain how I came to understand this I should perhaps give some further account of myself and my peculiar circumstances. During all the long, long years I have been seated here, ever since a most unpleasant night I spent shrouded beneath an extremely odor-iferous tarpaulin before darling Loosy came and superintended the replacing of it with a large Union Flag prior to our unveiling, I have become gradually, I must tell you, more and more aware of myself.

Now after so many years I have, I believe, a perfect recollection of all the events of my life up until our Coronation. That perhaps is to be expected. But I have as well acquired, more mysteriously, flashes of understanding of what happened to ourself after that time. At some moment, I cannot precisely say when, it was borne in on me, for instance, that I was created under the mallet and chisel of my own daughter, Louise, dearest Loosy, always skilful with her pencil and, as she advanced in years, under the encour-agement of my dear Albert – yes, a great deal of him has become known to me as I sit here – increasingly adept as a sculptress. My beloved Albert wrote once that sculpture is 'even more attractive than painting, because in it the thought is actually *incorporated*'. Little can he have realised how true those words of his have become in my own marble person.

I am able to remember, too – a most curious circumstance when one comes to think of it – all the further details of my unveiling here at this very spot by none other than ourself. It was, it seems, some fifty years later than the time of our Coronation, and the actual pulling at the cord which released the flag covering us was by the hand of – of whom? Well, of a stout gentleman of mature age whom I gathered was in fact my eldest son, Bertie, born to myself and dear, dear Albert some four years after the Coronation, some four years therefore after I came into my existence here.

So in this mysterious way I can recall – it must have been about the year '39 – reading Mr Charles Dickens's startling work *Oliver Twist*, from which I learnt something of the methods employed by the disgraceful young pickpockets working under the rule of that abominable creature, Fagin.

Fortified by my recollections of that exciting work, and thanks, too, to our often acknowledged powers of observation, I saw that the young man watched by myself and the lady on the bench was, beyond doubt, a pickpocket himself. But not at all a successful one. During the whole hour we observed him he failed time after time to secure any booty. And it was at each failure that my young companion, who eventually completely abandoned her book, slipping it into the reticule beside her, broke into that fleeting smile.

This is the sort of thing that happened. The young man spent some time walking more and more closely behind an obese individual disgracefully clad only in some sort of coloured cotton undervest and a pair of wide-cut trousers. From the back of these, one noticed after a little, there was protruding the top of a remarkably well-filled pocketbook. Eventually our young man appeared to need to pass in front of his target and, in doing so, trod heavily on his toe. Plainly he had intended at the same moment to slip the pocketbook from its place. But somehow he failed to bring hand and foot to the right points simultaneously. The fat man swung round, uttering an oath – happily too far off to come to our ears – and the youth, hardly apologising, rapidly made off.

Once during the course of the hour and more he was engaged in his nefarious activities he actually used ourself as a means of distracting one of his intended victims, a person I believed from his somewhat loud conversation with his wife to be an American visitor to our shores. The young pickpocket put on a pretence of being drunk and came weaving up to his victim, who was wearing his ostentatiously colourful jacket unbuttoned. The young man planted himself in front of the pair, flung out an arm vaguely in our direction and said in very loud tones: 'We are not amused. We are not amused.'

I had heard passers-by repeat this phrase on not a few occasions over the years I have been seated here, and I have gradually become aware that the words are supposed to have been said by ourself, though at a much later period of our life than our Kensington Palace days. We may have said them, once. I do not know. But I do know that they by no means represent our attitude to the passing show of life. I think some words I wrote in my youthful diary late one night after visiting the opera, there in my very bedroom not fifty yards distant now, better indicate our feelings. I had heard Grisi singing in Donizetti's *Anna Bolena*, and I wrote – I remember the precise words – 'I was VERY MUCH AMUSED INDEED.'

It was evident to me yesterday, repugnant though I found the young man's behaviour, that what he intended to do, under cover of our American visitor's embarrassment, was to reach inside his jacket and possess himself of the pocketbook there. However, the very loudness of his drunken impersonation so frightened the American's wife that he at once took her arm and marched her rapidly away. To the chagrin of the impolite young pickpocket. And ourself? We were very much amused.

On another occasion, again not far away from ourself, I saw the little-successful thief take from his own pocket a small pair of scissors. Coming quietly up behind a lady with a handbag dangling by a thin strap from her shoulder – one sees many such nowadays – he surreptitiously attempted to cut the bag's strap. Only to find his scissors too blunt. A fleeting smile might well have appeared then on our features, were they not carved in marble.

At other times during the young man's fruitless hour we, the lady on the bench and myself, were able to see him, by way of a preliminary exercise, tensely straightening the fingers of his right hand in order to make them into, as it were, a pair of human scissors. It was easy to guess his intent. Slip his extended hand into a gentleman's pocket, and, by means of those scissoring fingers, grip whatever was in there and gently slide it out. But, again, each time he approached a likely target something – perhaps even his heavy tread behind them or his failure to appear to avoid them from in front – caused the person in question to move away. The youth's subsequent frustration was plainly to be seen, even on occasion at a distance of fifty or sixty yards.

Eventually, baulked apparently of all further prey, he began to make his way towards the southern gate of the Gardens. But, just in front of us, he came to a sudden halt. And then he sauntered a pace or two forward – and how the forced casualness of that sauntering amused us – and, apparently seeing the bench there for the first time, with a great parade of fatigue he sat himself down on it at the other end from the young lady.

She, concealing I believe yet another smile, took her book out of her reticule again, leaving the latter, in a manner I thought to be most careless, gaping open beside her. Once more she plunged into its pages. I was, since the bench is several yards away, unable to see what the book's title was. But it occurred to me, so avidly did the young lady appear to be reading, that it might well be *Oliver Twist* itself or another of the engrossing works of Mr Dickens.

Time passed and I had begun to think I must look elsewhere for amusement this sunny afternoon. But then something – a small sudden movement – drew my attention again to the two young people on the bench. And I saw in an instant that the young man was now intent on sliding his hand into the girl's rather handsome reticule. It struck me that she must keep her purse in it, and that it was reprehensibly careless of her to leave it half-open in that manner when on the bench, just a foot or two away, there was a young man she knew to be a confirmed, if scarcely successful, pickpocket.

But, just as his hand slid to within an inch of the reticule, she happened, while still deep in the pages of her book, absent-mindedly to twitch it nearer herself.

I was able to note, out of the corner of my eye, the momentary expression of furious rage on the young man's not unhandsome countenance. He reminded me, indeed, of my cousin, young Prince Ferdinand of Saxe-Coburg, when he came with his father, my dear uncle, to visit us at Kensington on his way to marry the Queen of

Portugal, just a year before the death of my less dear Uncle William and all the great changes to our life which that brought about. Ferdinand had, much like this young man, a very slight figure with rather fair hair, beautiful dark brown eyes, a fine nose and a very sweet mouth, though of course I later found him by no means as handsome as my ever dear Albert. I well remember, however, a most merry and happy dinner at the Palace here with Ferdinand seated on my right. When he was not in company, he was, as I recall writing in our diary that night, 'most funny and childishly merry, which I delight in…'

I expected that the slight young man on the bench, after the rebuff his planned theft met with, however unintentional, would give up all further attempts. However, he made no move to leave.

My suspicions aroused by that, I directed my whole attention to the pair there.

Before long my vigilance was rewarded. I was able to see the young man, so like, despite his criminal tendencies, to dear Ferdinand as he was in those distant days, evidently assessing the distance between himself and my dark-haired young woman. He was estimating, it seemed, the exact angle at which she was sitting, still deeply absorbed in her reading, just where her elbow was, the very line of her outstretched feet. I have long despaired of the young people of today and their lack of any sense of decorum. However…

That young man intends at any minute, I said to myself, *to make a move.*

In a moment my guess proved right. He straightened up abruptly and peered hard into the distance.

'Hello, Sandra,' he called out, apparently to some acquaintance he had seen some way off. 'Sandra, hello!'

And then he leapt up and darted off, stumbling in his haste over the outstretched feet of the girl beside him.

She looked up furiously. But the young man, once more, failed to apologise and hurried away apparently in search of his friend.

But then I saw my young woman glance down at her right hand.

'My watch. The —'

I failed to make out what word it was she used about him, and perhaps it was as well.

But in any case my whole attention was fixed on the immediate chase she gave to the now-at-last successful thief. Happily, for me, he had made off in a direction encompassed by my unfortunately immovable gaze. So I was able to see the girl running, lightly as a veritable Atalanta, at a speed that soon brought her up to the pick-pocket, who at least had had the sense not to run from the scene of his crime in the way that poor, innocent young Oliver Twist ran from where the Artful Dodger and his friend Charley Bates had made off with the old gentleman's pocket handkerchief.

I was able to see her outpace her quarry and turn to confront him. I even saw that, rather than summoning a police constable – and, indeed, there was none about – she was holding out her hand as if demanding the immediate return of her stolen watch. I saw, too, that the thief was not responding to her request. Instead he seemed to be expostulating. No doubt he was attempting to make her believe she had chased altogether the wrong man.

However, plainly she knew too well what had happened, as from her observation of his activities for almost an hour before she could not but be. I saw her then point imperiously to the bench beside me where she had, in her haste, left her handsome leather reticule.

How unfortunate it is, I thought, that I am no longer under guard as I was, night and day, when I was first put in place. But at that time, now I suppose a hundred and thirty or forty years ago, no one had, after all, offered my unsullied marble any violence and the nightwatchman and the patrolling police had long ago been withdrawn. So there was no hope of someone taking care of that vulnerable reticule on, as it were, our behalf.

Such a precaution proved unnecessary, however. In less than two minutes the young lady came back, almost frogmarching the delinquent ahead of her.

'If you don't come nice and quietly,' I heard her say, 'I'm going to let out one tremendous scream and then accuse you of indecent assault. So if you don't want to get beaten up by every man around, you'd just better come with me.'

I was, I confess, a little perturbed at her tone, and her knowledge of the worser ways of the world. But that, alas, is something that all women have to learn about – one even did oneself – however little in my day it was customary to exhibit such knowledge.

In the present instance an attitude of some belligerence on the part of my fleet-footed friend proved to be all that was necessary. At the bench she quickly repossessed herself of her reticule and then indicated to her captive that he should sit down again where he had been before.

I prepared to give their encounter my fullest attention.

'All right,' she said, without preliminary. 'I want my watch back. Now. So no playing about, right?'

I could just see that the young man was sitting there saying nothing. What, evidently, I could not see was the look the young lady gave him then, though something in the set of her back allowed me an inkling of it.

It produced its result.

With a sheepish grin my latter-day Prince Ferdinand dipped his hand into his pocket and came out with the watch, dangling it by its thin leather strap.

'Thanks.'

She made to put it back on her wrist.

'Damn you. You've broken the strap.'

'Well, I had to, didn't I? You weren't going to hand it over just for the asking.'

'I was not. But that's neither here nor there. Thing is, you've broken it. And now you've got to pay for a replacement.'

I could see now the young man give her a broad, impudent grin.

'Won't be so easy that,' he said.

I realised then that, if my young female friend was of a certain class, the pickpocket, despite his informal but well-chosen clothes, was not.

But when the young lady answered him I began to realise something else. Something astonishing.

'Won't be easy to pay up because you haven't got a penny, have you?' she said.

'No. Not a bean.'

But it was not the words she used that astonished me. It was his attitude to her, and hers to him.

The fact of the matter, quite plainly, was that she was flirting with him. As he was with her, if a man can flirt. And she was a thief's victim, and he was that thief.

The banter between them progressed from there at a considerable rate. Very soon they were extremely mirthful, just as I believe young people ought to be. But I had to ask myself: was it right that two young people who were thief and victim should be merry? I found it a hard question to answer.

All the more so because a few minutes later I found that I myself had become the object of their mirth.

The young woman said something I was unable quite to catch. But she turned as she said it and pointed – pointed with outstretched finger – to ourself.

The young man looked up at me, directly into my face.

'Poor old duck,' he said. 'D'you think a bird done that streak right down her face?'

Without access to a looking-glass I had been unconscious of any such blemish, though for some considerable time past I had been just aware of a certain irregularity running down my right cheek.

But to have attention drawn to it in that thoroughly vulgar way...

I meditated how I could bring both of them to a sense of proper politeness.

But before any idea at all came to me the talk down on the bench again drew my attention.

'Yes,' the young woman said with sudden sharpness. 'You weren't telling me a word of a lie. You are totally penniless.'

And I saw that she was holding between her hands a worn black leather pocketbook, thin as a letterless envelope.

'Hey, that's mine. How did you...?

'Well,' came the answer, 'you're not the only pickpocket on the beach, my lad. And you're not the best either. Not by a long chalk.'

'But – but – Oh, Gawd, I done it now.'

'Done it? Oh, come on, you want to be a bit more lively than that.'

I saw her then give the boy a long, assessing inspection.

'You know, you're not bad-looking, not at all. And that can be pretty useful. When you're working a woman, for instance. Have her forget what she's about while she thinks what a dish you are, and a clever partner can have the necklace off her neck before she knows a thing about it.'

'You mean…? You mean, you and me?'

'Why not? Why not? You've got a lot to learn of course, but with a good teacher you'll be all right. One day.'

'Hey, then. It's partners?'

'Partners.'

I do not really know now whether we are amused or not.

# MRS CRAGGS
# AND THE LATE PRINCE ALBERT

When Mrs Craggs used to clean the Royal Albert Hall, or to be strictly accurate several offices within it, it was her habit leaving in the early morning, her work thoroughly done, to walk through the park to her second job of the day. Almost every time she did so she lingered at the Albert Memorial, climbing its many shallow steps and wandering round looking at all its myriad statues: the groups representing the Four Continents; the labelled groups representing the four pillars of prosperity, Agriculture, Manufacture, Commerce and Engineering; and the long four-sided panel of great men – a hundred and sixty-nine of them, she had counted – running all round the base.

She liked them all, the statues, though she had her favourites and her less favoured. A lot of effort had been put into making them and setting them round the great edifice which enshrouds the high tiny representation of the Consort himself, Albert the Good. She liked Albert, too. If by all he had done in life he had earned such mighty works as the Memorial and the massy circular Albert Hall, then, she thought, he must have been a hard worker too. And she honoured him for that.

So it was a matter of bitter regret to her for years and years that it was through her fault that bloody murder occurred one morning on the very steps leading up to the great man's Memorial.

It came about in this way. Every day as she made her tour of honour she used to see an odd trio of people hold a short meeting at the foot of the steps below. Two of them were identically tracksuited joggers and the third was a shortish, bald-headed man dressed invariably in overalls. The joggers would run up and wait, panting a little, till the man in overalls came walking up from the roadway, and then they would all three have some conversation, always very businesslike, usually quite brief, just sometimes more lengthy.

From the start their talk looked as though it was meant to be secret. But there was seldom anyone else nearby at that hour and somehow the three of them, having seen Mrs Craggs every day, soon discounted her presence and spoke quite loudly. In this way she got to know a good deal about the three and about the subject of their mysterious meetings.

The two joggers, she learnt, were brothers, a pair of lookalikes if ever there was. She even eventually got to know their names, Allingham and Bellingham Smith. Mr Allingham and Mr Bellingham, the third individual, whom Mrs Craggs knew only as the Technician, called them. Bel and Al they usually called each other.

Except for the occasions when Bellingham, who was quick and alert as the grey squirrels that scampered on the park paths nearby, called his brother in exasperation 'Albert'.

'Albert the Good, Albert the Dull,' Mrs Craggs heard him say once. And didn't like him any the better for it.

The subject of the clandestine meetings, Mrs Craggs bit by bit got to know, was something called the Heart Perpetuator. It seemed to be, as far as she could make out, a tiny thing you would wear clamped to your ribs which would not only keep an eye, or an ear, on your heart to detect the least, earliest sign of anything going wrong but also send little waves of something or other through your body that would at once put the trouble right.

The two brothers, who were scientists at Imperial College just down the road, were inventing it as a secret, out-of-hours project and the Technician was – their technician.

He was, in fact, the one who combined the different contributions of each brother – Bel has the brilliant ideas; Al was the one who got there by sheer hard thinking – into something real and solid, the prototype, as they called it when at last the whole secret enterprise neared completion.

In the long months while the device gradually approached this state, not without setbacks and dramas (these last particularly from the effervescent Bellingham), Mrs Craggs had grown extremely interested in the heart perpetuator. And this was what led in the end to murder.

Because all unwittingly one late morning at her second job, cleaning a very posh flat in Mayfair, she mentioned the magical machine to her employer. It was something to chat about, something she thought interesting. But to her surprise next day her employer's husband, a gentleman she had never seen before, questioned her closely about what she knew. She thought no more of it afterwards, except to reflect that some people had more time on their hands than they knew what to do with. And it was only a fortnight or so later, when she witnessed the terrific quarrel that broke out at the dawn meeting on the Memorial steps, that she realised, with a horrible sinking feeling, just what she had done.

The quarrel was, she understood in a moment, about a proposal by the Technician to leave Imperial College and go to the great multinational, Inter-Colloids, where as a newly made director of research he would set up a whole division to manufacture heart perpetuators, to be sold at a very high price to millionaires, oil sheikhs and captains of industry.

Mrs Craggs was outraged at the use that had been made of her. But the rest of the quarrel on the steps below was so interesting that she had to postpone thinking about that till some more convenient time.

The two brothers were each equally furious with the Technician. Darting Bellingham was enraged because he had seen the three of them setting up on their own much such a firm as the new division of Inter-Colloids. The sober, even dull, Allingham was angry because it had been his idea that they would simply send details of what they had perfected to something called 'the journals'. Mrs Craggs wasn't certain what these were, but she thought Allingham, Albert the Good, was right.

At that moment, however, sharp-eyed, squirrel-alert Bellingham spotted her and the three of them dropped into fierce undertones to continue their dispute.

And the next day the Technician was murdered.

Mrs Craggs saw it happen. Apparently he arrived at the morning trysting-place a little earlier than usual, before she got to the Memorial herself. But he was met not by both brothers jogging up to him but by one of them only. At a distance Mrs Craggs could not be sure which. But she could see quite clearly what it was he did.

He pulled a short sort of club from his tracksuit trousers and with a single blow to the Technician's bare, bald head felled him to the ground beside the Memorial's knobbed and spiked railing.

Mrs Craggs yelled out. She couldn't help it, although she was much too far away to be able to do anything. However, her single shocked cry must have been heard by the murderer because he looked round, saw her beginning to trundle forward at a run and took to his heels.

Of course, she couldn't possibly catch him. There were thirty years and more in age between them. So when she got to where the Technician lay she stopped, made sure that he was indeed dead and then went for a policeman.

There wasn't much she could say when she found a passing copper. But she had the satisfaction of thinking that she had at least alerted the forces of law and order as quickly as could be, and she trusted that they would do the rest.

It turned out her trust was not exactly rewarded.

Later that morning in the posh Mayfair flat, she learnt that a detective chief inspector wanted to see her. He proved to be a man she took against almost straight away. It was only because, heavily moustached and sullenly determined, his face reminded her at once of the rifle-carrying Plainsman from the Memorial group symbolising 'America', one of her least favourite of all the statues. She did her best to suppress the feeling. But she wasn't very successful.

Especially when Detective Chief Inspector America went on and on trying to make her say which of the brothers it was that she had seen. Right from the start she'd told him she couldn't at that distance tell one from the other. But he would go on. Just like, she thought, one of the park squirrels with a specially hard nut to crack.

At last, acknowledging her stone-wall refusal, he came out with what was the real source of his trouble.

'You see, this is what we call a premeditated affair,' he said, explaining with heavy patience. 'The weapon, that little club you saw, had actually been fashioned as an exact replica of one of the knobs on the Memorial railing. Given a minute or two more, our man would have nicely set up the death as some sort of curious accident. But, by the time we'd discovered where the brothers lived, in separate nearby flats as a matter of fact, first we found Mr Bellingham Smith still in bed and drugged to the wide – had to break in, tell the truth – then, when we went to Mr Allingham Smith's, it turned out to be exactly the same with him.'

Mrs Craggs looked unbelieving.

'Well, of course,' Detective Chief Inspector America went on, 'one of them was faking it, one had doped his brother and gone off and done the murder and then had come back and doped himself. But – keep this to yourself, mind – we're damned if we can tell which. Not the officers who saw them first. Not the police surgeon. Not me.'

The outraged squeak with which he delivered these last two words from behind his thickly curving moustaches put Mrs Craggs in the picture straight away. Unless Chief Inspector America could sort out which of the two brothers had used that deadly cosh and which one had, innocently drugged, slept through the whole time of the crime, he would be unable to make an arrest.

She thought for a second or two, eyes tight closed.

Then she told the grimly determined chief inspector what he wanted to hear.

'You know which of 'em it really was, don't you?' she said, though she was perfectly well aware that he was thoroughly stumped.

Chief Inspector America remained silent. But slowly above his ponderous moustaches his cheeks went a dull red.

'Supposing you – er – give me your opinion,' he said at last.

'It's not opinion,' Mrs Craggs answered. 'It's plain downright fact.'

'Your fact then. If you'd be so good.'

'Albert,' said Mrs Craggs then, with a long, long sigh. 'It was Albert the Good, Albert the Dull.'

'Albert? But neither of them's called –'

'Oh, Allingham then, if you must have it all correct.'

'Allingham? But why? From what I've heard from you and others Bellingham's the one with the brains.'

'Not a bit of it. My Albert the Good's every bit as high-powered in the brain-box department. It's just that he's the painstaking one. The one that's got to get everything right before he settles for it. If it'd been Bellingham what done the murder, he'd have just killed that nasty greedy man and then tried to talk his way out of it afterwards.'

'Well,' said Chief Inspector America, 'it's true we did find a phial of a highly toxic chemical Bellingham apparently had misappropriated from Imperial College when we searched his flat. And we were thinking of arresting him on the strength of that, if you couldn't come up with a proper identification.'

He put a large red hand up in front of his moustache and coughed.

'I suppose in view of what you've just disclosed you wouldn't care to identify Allingham Smith now?' he asked.

'I would not,' said Mrs Craggs.

'No, I thought you wouldn't. So what am I to do? What you've told me isn't what we in the police call good evidence, you know.'

'No, I suppose it ain't,' Mrs Craggs said. 'So now you want to know how you can pin it fair and square on poor old Albert?'

'Yes,' said Chief Inspector America quite simply.

So Mrs Craggs told him.

And, of course, when the chief inspector pretended to arrest the brilliant Bellingham, Allingham, Albert the Good, Albert the Dull, promptly confessed.

# INCIDENT AT MILLIONAIRES' ROW

The private road, called officially Kensington Palace Gardens, that runs down the west side of one of London's royal parks is more commonly known as Millionaires' Row. It is lined by a number of huge houses with their backs looking out on the wide green stretch and towering old trees of Kensington Gardens themselves. In their time these mansions – they are nothing less – have belonged to fabulously wealthy maharajahs, have housed the ultra-secret embassy of the Soyuz Sovetskikh Sotsialisticheskikh Respublik, have numbered among them even the residence of a television mogul.

So perhaps it should be a matter of no surprise that early one morning in the late winter of the year 199– two police motorcyclists should come at full speed, sirens yowling, one after another along the Bayswater Road and turn with squealing tyres through the mildly crumbling stone gateway that leads into this most discreet of discreet thoroughfares. Or that, minutes later, they were followed by a police car flashing its blue lamp.

Outside the residence of the Ambassador of a certain Arab state, which had better be nameless, they halted. The enormous front door of the building opened. Giving each other fractionally nervous glances, the helmeted, yellow-jerkined motorcyclists, outriders of a team from the Diplomatic Protection Group, entered the building. To be greeted in the high marbled hallway by the sight of the Ambassador himself, apoplectic with fury, striding back and forth, brandishing a small camel-whip and apparently incapable, in the enormity of the crisis he was experiencing – whatever it was – of bringing himself to use the barbarous language of his host nation.

In the background, distinctly subdued and hardly daring to look at one another, a dozen members of the Ambassador's staff, ranging from secretaries to cooks, watched in terrified helplessness.

However, with the arrival a minute or two later of the car bringing the Group's night-duty officer, Detective Inspector Greenmoor, His Excellency contrived to abate his fury enough to communicate at least an outline of the monstrous trouble that had befallen him.

'He is in there. There.'

The little camel-whip was pointed, quivering, at a stout, gleamingly polished tall door towards the back of the hall.

'I see, sir. Yes. But may I – er – inquire whom you are referring to?'

'No. Yes. No. Mr Inspector, these policemen do they understand Arabic?'

Inspector Greenmoor peered at the faces under the ballooning yellow helmets.

'No, sir. Unfortunately neither of them speaks any of your language, as far as I am aware.'

'Good, good, Mr Inspector. And you? Do you speak Arabic?'

'Well, sir, I can manage a word or two. Part of my duties as you might say.'

There followed from the ambassadorial mouth a stream of language from which the two motorcycle men, hands resting lightly on their revolver holsters, were able only to make out that the Ambassador was still in an almighty rage.

Inspector Greenmoor, though a good deal foxed by the speed and volume of the outpouring, thought he had grasped at least the essentials of the situation.

The Ambassador, a Prince of the royal blood, had, it appeared, been entertaining for the night at this, his private residence, an envoy from a neighbouring Arab country usually at daggers drawn with his own.

A piece of vigorous involuntary mime had helped the Inspector here.

Negotiations, he had gathered, were taking place. A huge change of alliances was in the air. No one must know. 'Most secret, Mr Inspector, ten thousand per cent.'

The Ambassador had fallen into English for that. But the rest of his explanation was in even faster, more furious Arabic, and Inspector Greenmoor's scanty knowledge of the tongue almost completely failed him.

But it seemed that earlier that morning the visitor, a distant relation in fact of his host – 'cousin, cousin, just, just, you understand?' – had kidnapped the Ambassador's small daughter and was holding her, perhaps to ransom, in the room with the heavy, well-polished door.

'Well, sir,' the Inspector said, descending to his own language, 'Commander Holsworthy, H.O.D.P.G., that is – er – Head of the Diplomatic Protection Group, is on his way, I am pleased to say. But perhaps it would be worthwhile, just now, me trying the door of the room.'

'As you wish, as you wish.'

Inspector Greenmoor went over to the door, gently turned the massive brass handle, gently pushed. Locked. He ventured a polite tap on one of the gleaming panels.

'Go away,' said a childish voice in Arabic.

'Are you well and happy?' Inspector Greenmoor ventured in the same language.

'Go away.'

'It looks as if the poor little girl may be under some sort of threat, sir. I think perhaps we had better wait till Commander Holsworthy arrives.'

'Wait, wait, wait. All the time it is waiting, waiting. Never acting, acting. I must speak to my cousin. Now, now. And not through any door.'

'Yes, sir.'

At that moment, much to Inspector Greenmoor's relief, his superior arrived, in a suitably superior motor vehicle. And in full, braid-sparkling uniform.

A quick word at the door and he was put in the picture.

'Your Excellency, this is a most unfortunate business. However, I am reasonably fluent in your language, and perhaps I may be able to persuade your cousin to release your little daughter.'

This provoked a yet more torrential and enraged outpouring. But when comparative calm had descended at last, Commander Holsworthy, who had succeeded only in interjecting a very occasional question, went over and had a quiet word with his deputy.

'Seems you got the wrong end of the stick a bit, John. What's happened here apparently, if you can believe it, is not that the Ambassador's cousin has kidnapped his daughter, but that the little girl, who's aged just eleven, has kidnapped him. She's got him locked in the dining-room there, and nothing her father can say will make her open the door.'

'But why, sir? What on earth's the idea?'

'Nobody seems to know. Least of all her father. Still, he's agreed to let me have a go. So perhaps a rather more diplomatic approach... But what I want you to do is talk to the Ambassador.'

'Yes, sir. Er – What about?'

'Oh, come on, John. About anything. Anything. So long as he doesn't come barging in, cracking that whip of his, while I'm doing my stuff.'

Inspector Greenmoor gulped. Once. And marched over to the Ambassador.

'This – er – Well, Your Excellency, I believe this is the first time you've had occasion to call on our services.'

'What? What is that? That man – your Head of whatever it is – what is he saying?'

Greenmoor had heard two quiet taps on the heavy, locked door followed at once by an indignant squeaked 'Go away' in Arabic. And now there was a stream of gently inflected Arabic, Egyptian variation, in reply. But luckily too far away for the words to be made out.

The Ambassador started out in its direction.

Inspector Greenmoor went so far as to put a hand on his arm.

'As I was saying, Your Excellency... That is, what was I saying? Oh, yes, I was about to ask you – about to ask you if... if you had any recommendations about our work? Yes. I mean, are you satisfied with the guard we keep at the embassy itself? We're always ready to listen to the people we have the – er – pleasure of serving. Any ideas of – er – that sort?'

'No.'

'I see, Your Excellency. Then – Then we must be doing all right. Yes. Well, I'm pleased to hear that. But –'

A tug at the hand on the ambassadorial arm.

'One moment more, Your Excellency, if I may. We don't often get an opportunity of hearing whether our services...'

Then, at last, the sound of a small female voice speaking in what seemed to be an altogether reasonable manner from directly on the other side of the tall door.

More Egyptian Arabic.

Was there a wheedling note in it? Or was it just that Arabic sounded like that?

'As I was saying. Your Excellency...'

And, unbounded relief, the click of a heavy door being unlocked.

Inspector Greenmoor whirled round.

A small and very pretty Arab girl came out, leading by the hand an impeccably distinguished young man in white djellaba and white headdress. She was smiling up at her captive in a manner that, in two or three years' time, would be nothing short of open invitation.

'Uncle is very, very nice,' she said in clear, if slightly childish English, addressing the assembled representatives of the Metropolitan Police as much as the still cringing members of the Ambassador's household at the far end of the hall. 'I had to have him for myself, just for a bit. There was too much talking and talking all the time.'

The sound that emanated from her father at this could only be described as a snarl of pure rage.

'Come here,' he shouted in a voice that reverberated and reverberated from the marble walls all around.

'No, Your Excellency,' Commander Holsworthy snapped in. 'I very much regret to inform you that it is my duty to place your daughter under arrest.'

31

'Under arrest? Under arrest? Mr Policeman, have you gone mad?'

'No, Your Excellency. A crime has been committed, the serious offence of kidnap. The culprit must be brought to justice.'

'Mr Policeman, this is my house, my country's territory. I shall exercise whatever justice is to be done.'

And the little camel-whip was brought down with an almighty thwack on the top of a conveniently placed buhl chiffonier.

'Well, no, Your Excellency, that's not quite the situation,' Commander Holsworthy replied. 'Perhaps it has slipped your memory that this is not your country's Embassy, which of course is out of our jurisdiction, but it is simply your private house. So I am afraid I have no alternative but to take this young lady into custody.'

Before the Ambassador had quite finished drawing himself up to his full height, Commander Holsworthy had ushered his 'collar' out of the wide front door.

Inspector Greenmoor, at a nod of command, got into the back of the Commander's car, sliding the young criminal in beside him.

'The Yard, Jenkins,' Commander Holsworthy said to his driver, slipping inside in his turn.

Smoothly the car took off. Only when they had turned into the Bayswater Road did Inspector Greenmoor venture to lean across the small figure between them.

'With respect, sir,' he said. 'Wasn't that a bit – well, high-handed? Not exactly diplomatic, you might say?'

'Yes, John. In one way it was. On the other hand, you could say I was exercising to the full the duties of the Diplomatic Protection Group. Using what you might call a little adroit diplomacy to protect this young lady's backside.'

# BLOOD AND BONE

In the summertime Mr G.R. Cann, having had his bite of breakfast, left the house where he had his small flat each day at exactly 7
a.m. and walked up to Kensington Gardens. In the winter dark he
rose later and went to the public library where he spent the morning in the reading room with the papers, thereby saving himself
some expense. But really he preferred when he could to digest the
pages of the *Daily Mail*, bought at the newsagent opposite, in the
comparative solitude of the garden at the Orangery, on a shaded
bench if it was fine, inside if wet.

He always took the same route, too, from May to October. This
passed, as it happened, a shop – it had been there as long as Mr
G.R. Cann could remember – bearing the sign *Ironmonger   G.R.
Cann   Domestic Stores*. About a hundred yards from it, Mr G.R.
Cann always crossed over to the far pavement. He did not like it to
be thought that he was making himself out to be more than he was
because of the coincidence of the names. But the shop was on his
most direct way to the park, and he felt, too, it would be wrong to
go round by another route.

From that far pavement, however,  he invariably gave the shop's
crowded window a quick glance. He had remarkably good sight
still, needing spectacles only for reading, and was generally able to
see whether any new stock had been put on display. Of course, he
had never ventured inside the place. He felt that, on account of the
similarity of names, it would be somehow wrong. But he liked to
assure himself that trade was healthy.

And on this particular day, a day he was long to remember,
he saw from across the width of the street that trade was, indeed,

flourishing, although he wished that it could have flourished in some other way. Because at some time on the previous day the proprietors had filled one third of the shop's small window with what must have been, he thought, a bargain bulk purchase. It was of large packets labelled in bright red letters *Blood and Bone*.

Mr G.R. Cann realised in a moment that the packets contained nothing else than garden fertiliser. But for just one instant he had been deeply upset by them. He disliked violence. He disliked even the thought of it. It shattered the order of things. And the blood-red words on the packets, however horticultural a moment's thought had shown them to be, had said to him with sudden inexorability: violence.

But in a minute or so, back on his proper side of the street, he was able to make his way at his customary sedate pace, taking in the various regular events that lay in his path and finding his customary pleasure in them. There was the place where, day after day, he heard the gurgle of water in the drainpipe running down the side of a big mansion block indicating that some unknown person had just emerged from a morning bath. There was the compulsively talkative old lady who contrived to come out to the milkman every day just as his float halted at the corner of the wide stretch of Palace Court. There was the burly man, filling in the *Times* crossword as he walked head down, who almost always came out of the park gates just as Mr G.R. Cann himself went in.

Mr G.R. Cann knew that he could not always rely on encountering each of them at the same place every day, but it gave him a little lift when such signs of regularity and order manifested themselves. He would have liked the world always to stay as it was, with whatever was there, good or bad, never changing. But he knew that change did come. After all, it was at very little notice that he had to leave the desk he occupied for years at Mayhew and Mayhew, glass merchants. He knew that there had to be changes, and he had brought himself to accept that.

And change, he found that day, had come even to early-morning Kensington Gardens, subject usually only to the changing pattern of the seasons. But there now, cutting off the broad path leading down to the Orangery, was a long fence of chestnut palings sweeping out in a wide arc from the neat iron railing that separates the public area from the lawn where royalty and its servants from time to time jump horses or play football.

Mr G.R. Cann guessed at once why the fence was there. A similar arrangement had been made as a security measure some years before when a particularly vulnerable President of the United States had come to London. And now an equally vulnerable visitor, or one even more so, was due to arrive. Mr G.R. Cann had read about him in the *Daily Mail*. It was Dr Prigono, President of Vorneo, the Vulture of Vorneo the *Mail* called him. Not without justice, if even half what they said about him was true. Innocent people shot by the hundred. What they called torture camps set up by the dozen, with Dr Prigono often personally supervising what went on in them. A thoroughly nasty piece of work. And coming to Britain, apparently, to sign some multi-million arms deal. There had been an outcry. Protest marches. A group of Vornean exiles had started a riot outside the Embassy. But the Government had persisted. Jobs, it was said, were at stake.

But now, standing beside the notice saying *Please Encourage Your Dog to Use This Enclosure and Not Foul Other Areas of the Park* – a notice he always liked for its tone of quiet politeness – and taking in the full extent of the protective zone of chestnut palings, Mr G.R. Cann thought he understood what was happening. The Vulture of Vorneo was, according to the *Mail,* not due to come to Britain till next week. But, plainly, his arrival had been secretly advanced to forestall the protests, and the long stretch of palings had been put up overnight as an extra precaution.

Mr G.R. Cann hoped the Government knew what they were about, though. In his experience at Mayhew and Mayhew, if you altered arrangements at the last moment – Young Mr Bob had been a great one for doing that, full of sudden enthusiasms – things were apt to go wrong. People who needed to know were not informed, or sometimes the other way about. And then there was muddle.

Well, he thought, it's none of it anything to do with me. I'll just have to go the long way round to the Orangery. Can't be helped.

Just then one of his regulars came swooping by, the young fat lady with her three little brownish dogs. And, yes, he saw as she waddled rapidly away, the bright-coloured skirt that hung from her waist like a circular curtain still had that place at the back where the hem had come adrift. He had noticed it first three days ago. Not much that got past him unless he was wearing his reading specs. And the young miss was failing to *encourage her dogs to use*. As per usual.

Somewhat heartened by this example of regularity, even if in a bad cause, Mr G.R. Cann set out again, heading for his customary bench among the huge, still, calming, clipped trees lining the central walk of the Orangery garden. And, as he skirted the obtrusive palings, he saw ahead of him another of his regulars. A comparatively new planet in the regular circlings of the earliest park walkers, but a regular for all that. A man in a fawn raincoat who had come at this time every day for the past month exercising a big borzoi. There he was now, marching along as ever – he always *encouraged the borzoi to use*, waiting patiently while it sniffed among the sand until it had found a spot it was happy with – the dog's lead dangling from one hand and his stout walking-stick swinging like a pendulum from the other.

Mr G.R. Cann began to feel that, despite the palings and what they signified, all was as right with the world as could reasonably be expected.

And then, coming with a sudden blotting-out roar of sound seemingly from out of a cloudless sky, a helicopter was descending on to the royal lawn. All the passers-by stopped and stood stock-still, staring, as if the noise and wild motion inside the palings had to be compensated for in complete stillness and silence outside them – the fat young lady with the dropped skirt-hem, even her dogs were frozen in stillness, the man walking the borzoi, the joggers Mr G.R. Cann had hardly yet noticed, though he knew the girl all in white would have on her tee-shirt, as it had every morning for more than a month, the slogan *Swedish Secret*.

He had never quite understood what that meant. But there were lots of things in today's world he did not really understand.

And now the helicopter was down. From the royal residence at the end of the lawn a small group of men in black tailcoats began approaching. The wide doors of the helicopter were thrust open. Steps were lowered. And then, there in the doorway, lit by the bright morning sun, stood a huge man in a uniform that made those of the cinema commissionaires Mr G.R. Cann remembered from his youth look like models of decorum. Gold glittered from two massive epaulettes. It glinted from twined braid across the chest. It shone like a halo all round the brilliant blue cap. And the man simply stood there, like a conquering hero. A hero who, despite all the evil he had done, was conquering this feeble, desperate-for-money island on whose soil he had just arrived.

The Vulture of Vorneo stood there. But out of the corner of his eye, Mr G.R. Cann, standing modestly at the rear of the cluster of spectators, saw one single quiet movement among the statue-struck, silent group. It was only afterwards that he fully realised what that slow movement was. It was the man with the borzoi, not ten yards away from him, slowly raising his heavy walking-stick till it pointed straight at the gold-dazzling figure in the helicopter doorway.

And then, quite suddenly, the full brown face under the glinting braided cap exploded. Into a hurling outwards of blood and bone.

Mr G.R. Cann actually saw the bone. White fragments. With his excellent long-sight he was able to make them out quite clearly, shooting outward together with the bright red blood.

Perhaps it was the sheer vividness of the sight that stopped him, after one involuntary step towards the man with the deadly walking-stick, from doing anything more. But it was not shock that, a second later, kept him standing just where he was. It was – he came to realise thinking about it all later that morning – a conscious decision. He had decided to suspend judgement.

At the end of half a minute the officials, whoever they were, on board the helicopter had leapt into action. Scarcely had the Vulture's body tumbled forward to lie inert on the English grass below than four or five uniformed men came jumping down after him. One crouched over the body as if there could be any doubt that it was body, a dead body. The others knelt, weapons suddenly in their hands, in a defensive shield all round.

And the spectators began to react as well, in a dozen different ways. The girl with the *Swedish Secret* tee-shirt set up a tiny, high-pitched screaming that went on and on like a burglar alarm. The fat young woman collapsed plump-down among her little brown dogs. Two of the joggers ran forward to the palings, looking as if they were going to vault over, and then when they saw that semi-circle of pointing guns threw themselves flat. From further off others of the park's early birds began hurrying towards the scene. But the man with the borzoi simply stood where he was, stick by his side, looking at the helicopter and the big sprawled body in front of it, for all the world as if it was a sight of some interest but nothing more. A minor street accident. A scuffle between two or three youths.

Mr G.R. Cann wondered whether he ought to go up to him and carry out a citizen's arrest. It was not any fear of what other bullets there might be in that disguised gun that kept him back. Nor did he even feel that an arrest was something that ought to be left to officialdom. A police officer in uniform from among the black tail-coats at the royal residence was coming purposefully across now. But Mr G.R. Cann was sure that no one knew it was the man with the stick who should be arrested. No one else, he was certain, would have noticed that slow raising-up of the stick gun, its equally slow lowering after the blood and bone had spurted out.

No, he felt simply that the matter needed more consideration.

And he knew, too, that there was no need for hurry. The man with the borzoi was not going to make a sudden break for it. Not from the way he was standing there, quietly looking on. In fact, in all probability at this same time next morning he would be there once again. He would put his dog into the enclosure and wait, quite patiently, until it had chosen to perform. And then he would resume his walk, going down to the Round Pond, exactly where he had gone yesterday, exactly where he had gone on all the mornings for the past month.

Because, Mr G.R. Cann had come to realise with a slow, placid dawning of understanding, the dog-walker was a professional assassin. A hit-man.

It must have been an extraordinarily well thought-out affair. No doubt the man had been recruited by those exiles who had rioted the other day outside the Embassy, and, once engaged, he had set about his job in a thoroughly professional manner. The point had been to establish himself as a regular visitor to the park, someone who had a right to be where he was when he was. So he would have got hold of a dog, and one that was particularly noticeable, and begun his regular walks with it, swinging his heavy walking-stick, past the place where the American President had once landed and where – no doubt the exiles had their sources of information – it was expected the Vulture would land in his turn. And the rest had been simple. Daring but simple.

One of the newcomers was helping the fat young woman to her feet now, collecting the dusty trailing leads of her little dogs, asking her evidently whether she felt all right. And a moment or two later she was setting off back in the direction of the gates. A shorter walk than usual for three small brown dogs. The flat-on-their-faces joggers were scrambling to their feet, looking rather ashamed. Only in the far distance there could be heard the wail of police sirens. The man with the borzoi turned and began to walk away in the direction of the Round Pond.

Mr G.R Cann decided there was no reason to linger either. He set off towards the calm of the massive clipped trees of the Orangery garden. There was nothing he could say to help the police when they arrived. Other, of course, than to tell them who it was who has sent the Vulture's head fanning out in that mixture of blood and bone. And he had not made up his mind yet whether he would do that. After all, there were people who were better dead. You could not let the world go on and on for ever in its bad old way. He needed to think it all out. In his own time.

# OLD PETE

'But – But –' the shabby, greasy old man said, 'I need the work.'

Behind the paper-strewn acres of his desk, Butler Rogers simply sat in silence. Puffed scarlet cheeks set in two inflexible downward curves, little bright blue eyes hard as a pair of stony carbuncles.

'Haven't you got anything?' the old man said at last, wiping the end of his big, hungry-looking nose and giving a loud sniff. 'I mean, I've done a lot for you. Over the years. I can remember when Rogers Investigations was just you and a desk in that room of yours off Chancery Lane.'

'Over the years, over the years. What you forget, you miserable old bugger, is how many of those years there've been. Frankly, I wouldn't want you to do a job for me now if you were the last operative in the world.'

'But I need – I must have the money. I must have it.'

'Well, you're not getting any from me. What you want money for anyhow, your age?'

'I got my needs. That's all. My needs. And they ain't no business of – of – of anybody's.'

'Oh, your big secret. You don't think everybody who's ever worked alongside you don't know about that. Porno mags. You disgust me. You really disgust me.'

'All right, I like a bit o' porn, and why shouldn't I? Plenty of people do. I dare say you look at a mag or two yourself, time to time.'

'What if I do? It don't mean I spend every penny I've got on 'em. It don't mean I go begging and whining for a job just so as I can go and get myself some new bit o' filth. You ought to grow up, you ought.'

The old man looked down at the carpet – thick, rich brown, client-impressing. His shoes, their scuffed leather grey from lack of polish, rays of white cracks all over.

'I got an addiction, see. People get 'em. Addictions. Fags, drink, cocaine. Well, mine's the books. An' the price of 'em nowadays…'

'Should cure you then, you nasty old sod. No, go away. Grow up. I got nothing for you. Nothing.'

'But I'm good, Butl – I'm good, Mr Rogers. You know I am.'

'Were, Pete. Were. You were good, once. I grant you that. Very neat with the snatched photo, good as anybody. Once.'

'I still got my old camera, Mr Rogers. I could still use it. Picture sharp as could be.'

'Yeah, and the subject smell you a mile off, you old creep. You know what I do, minute you leave my room? I call in my young girl – Wendy, I call her Bendy Wendy, get it? – and I have her open all the windows and give the place a good puffing with her little squirter.'

'I can't help it if I pong a bit. You wait till you're as old as me. And as poor.'

'Then stop buying all them mags an' get yourself a bar of soap. Go on, now. Out.'

'But, Mr Rogers, I'm still good, good as ever I was. I won't get near the subject, not within yards. I was always first-class with the dogging. You know that.'

'Dogging? Dogging? Listen, old-timer. We don't do dogging in the trade no more. Tailing. It's tail – Hey, wait a minute, though. I just might –'

The two bright blue eyes flicked here and there over the mess of papers on the big glossy desk. Stopped. Alighted. Podgy pink hands flipped at the pile, extracted a letter. Thick, dark blue writing-paper.

'Yeah. Look, I'll give you this. Since you're a dogger.'

An unpretty grin. Blue eyes swivel to fasten on Old Pete's lank, unshaven face.

'It's not much of a job, mind. Don't know why I took it on really. Fee's not going to pay for all the correspondence, hardly.'

'No, but I'll do it, Butler. I won't put in for expenses. Just the usual'll suit me. Just the usual.'

The look of eagerness in the bleary eyes with the horny yellow scales at the sides. Pathetic.

'Yeah, well, it was dogging that made me think of it. Old geezer here –' He tapped the stiff blue sheet with one bitten-short nail. 'Thinks his young missus is seeing some man. He's never been able to cotton on to where they meet. But he's decided it's got to be when she takes her doggie for a walk, first thing in the morning. Kensington Gardens. Wants proof.'

'Kensington Gardens. Won't be the first job I done there. Cor, yes, I remember three or four years back it was. When I was working regular.'

'More like ten years then, fifteen. You ain't worked regular, Pete, more years than I can count.'

'Well, maybe it was longer than that. But I remember it. Same as if it was yesterday. Some bloody parent, South Ken way. Wanted to know what her fat little daughter was getting up to, hours late back from school. Laying right on top of him, she was, all in her pretty school uniform. And wriggling. Wriggling something chronic.'

'A schoolgirl, you nasty old perv. Go on, get out of my sight. Here's the old idiot's address, Gloucester Terrace. Girl trots out with the pooch, half-past seven every morning, regular as clockwork, so he says.'

Old Pete took the scrawled piece of paper, glanced at it.

'I'll need the flat number,' he said. 'Those big houses there, they're all divided into flats nowadays.'

Butler Rogers looked momentarily put out. Then he blustered.

'If there'd been a flat number I'd have given it you, wouldn't I, you old fool? It's the whole house, I told you, didn't I? Now, get out. Go on, push off.'

Old Pete began heaving himself to his feet.

'Wendy, Wendy,' Butler Rogers shouted. 'Where is that damn girl? Always bloody trying to mother me when I don't want her, and when I do... I'll give her Bend – Ah, there you are, sweetheart. Bring in your flowery squirt, will you? Pete here's just leaving.'

Just after seven o'clock next morning a slouching old man in a long black overcoat who might have been a vagrant or a beggar of some sort, carrying a battered old brown leather shopping-bag, was to be seen making his way along Gloucester Terrace, just barely glancing at the tall doorways of the houses he passed with their panels of multiple bellpushes to one side or another. He did not change his dragging pace when he went by the second house from the end where, in place of a panel of bells, there was just one, a big, fat white button, its brass surround glinting in the bright morning sunshine. But at the top of the road he crossed over and put himself, a flapping scarecrow, into the deserted bus-stop shelter there.

He waited. A Number 94 rounded the corner. He stepped back. The bus halted. Its conductor looked out for an instant, rang his bell. The bus ground away from the stop. The old man shuffled forward again.

Then almost exactly at half-past seven the door of the house with the well-polished bell opened and a young woman came out. She was casually dressed in jeans and a beige checked shirt, and, lolloping down the steps after her, there came a big lumbering dog.

St Bernard, Old Pete murmured knowledgeably to himself.

He watched them go past opposite, cross to the big triangular traffic island and wait for a gap in the stream of early-morning cars along the Bayswater Road, the dog sitting patiently beside the woman. Idly, head down, he set off for the island himself.

He had only just stationed himself on the Bayswater Road kerb at the far end when a gap came in the flow of the traffic.

'Off we go, Nana,' the young woman said to the dog, her clear, confident voice easily reaching Old Pete's ears.

Not a dog, a bitch then, he said to himself as he, too, set out across the road.

He had to scurry the last two or three yards as the next wave of traffic bore down at him. But the errant wife – if such she was – and the big white dog were well within sight when he sidled through the tall gate into the Gardens.

Won't be no difficulty dogging that one, he thought to himself. If I miss her, St Bernard'll be easy to spot quarter of a mile off. Not that I'm likely to miss that little piece o' goods. Pity I ain't taking no porno pic of her. Nice ladylike sort, adds a touch of extra spice.

Ahead, the girl strode confidently along past the Italian Garden, the big St Bernard trotting sedately at her heel. Fifty or sixty yards behind, Old Pete shuffled along in his turn, his ancient brown leather shopping-bag – with the little hole cut in the front for the lens of his camera – swinging dolefully in his hand. He glanced over the railing at the benches surrounding the four wide rectangular basins, their fountains not playing at this early hour, the water tranquil if slimy green.

Pity it isn't there she meets this young man of hers, if he ain't all in the old husband's bloody imagination, Pete thought. But where'd I be if it turns out like that? No pic, no pay. An' I must have the price of a few o' those new books I saw in the shop when I had a browse around. I just must. Sod old Butler with his *Grow up*. If I like 'em, why shouldn't I have 'em?

An early-morning runner came up, went past, the sound of his hoarse breathing clear in the fresh morning air.

The girl and the dog were still forging ahead, now along the path following the edge of the Longwater. Old Pete mended his pace a little as the bushes of the railed-off shrubbery on the other side of the path momentarily took them out of view.

*Dogs must be kept on leash in this area,* a notice at the corner of the shrubbery discreetly proclaimed.

Didn't see no lead with the St Bernard, Pete muttered. She ought to obey the regulations, nice young girl like that.

He rounded the corner.

And managed to drift to a stop when he saw that, just opposite the Peter Pan statue, the girl had halted. Beside her the big dog settled down comfortably on her haunches.

Used to waiting here, are you then, Peter said to himself. So this is the meeting place. Her young man coming up from the other side of the Gardens, by the look of it. Way she's sitting on that bench there now and glancing all the time in that direction while she's making out she's watching the little new ducklings swimming about in the lake.

He put his bag down on the ground and pretended to be rustling about for something inside. In the empty interior his camera nestled as always, lens fixed to the hole at the front, film in place, setting at the twenty yards he liked to work at, ready adjusted for the bright sun.

Then the St Bernard gave a sudden, single, joyful bark. Pete looked up out of the corner of his eye. A young man had just rounded the bend at the far end of the shrubbery, much the same age as the girl, curly-headed, fresh-faced, blue jeans and a bright white, red-striped shirt.

The dog hurried up to him, jumped up and put her paws on his chest, wagging her stump of a tail like a steam-engine.

'Good dog, Nana. Good dog.'

He put her down and the pair of young lovers rushed into each other's arms. And stayed there.

Bugger it, Old Peter snarled to himself, light's all wrong this direction or I could of done it right away from just where I am. Better try getting in the shrubbery here instead and come up just behind that statue, see what I can do from behind a bush. Ought to be a gate in the railings somewhere. Don't much relish the thought of getting over, not at my age.

He picked up his bag and set off at a much faster pace than when he had been an old vagrant wandering by chance in the same direction as a pretty young woman and her big St Bernard. In a minute or so he found a gate open in the railings at the back of the shrubbery where a wide path led to a clearing used by the Gardens staff to keep machinery out of sight. There was a notice forbidding entry, but he paid no attention to it.

In the end he had to force his way cautiously through some yards of brambly undergrowth. But in less than two minutes he was within sight of the bronze pyramid of the Peter Pan statue with its entwined fairy children clambering eagerly up towards the ethereal form of the Boy Who Never Grew Up in his wispy inverted flower-bell tunic, striding out bare-legged into the unknown, his ever silent pipe at his lips. And just in front were the two lovers, still happily locked in each other's arms.

'Oh, Wendy, Wendy, Wendy,' the young man murmured through her curtain of hair.

And 'Michael, Michael, Michael,' she murmured back.

Old Pete licked his lips, and murmured too. 'Cor, what wouldn't I give, see the pair of 'em bollock naked.'

His voice must have been louder than he had meant it to be. Or perhaps a fleeting puff of breeze had sent his strong odour, much complained of by Butler Rogers, floating down towards the lake. For whatever reason, Nana, the big dog, suddenly rose to her feet from where she had been quietly lying, eyes only a blink open, and stood, growling steadily. And pointing directly to the spot where he was just getting his camera up to take aim through the viewfinder.

Christ, he thought, she'll be over the railings and come for me. Great big hound like that.

He shoved the camera back into the bag he had dropped at his feet, blundered round and, careless now of how much noise he might be making, headed for the open gate and safety.

Or, comparative safety. Because he decided at once that he was not going to linger anywhere near. Supposing the youngster had got a glimpse of him. In no time at all he could sprint round the shrubbery, and then what wouldn't he do to someone he thought was a Peeping Tom.

Next morning, however, a man in a long black overcoat who might have been a vagrant or a beggar of some sort, carrying a battered leather shopping-bag, was standing in the deserted bus shelter at the top of Gloucester Terrace. But as soon as he saw the door open in the house with the big fat bellpush and a young woman come out with a bumbling white dog beside her, he turned away and succeeded in getting across the busy Bayswater Road before the pair had even reached the traffic island.

Inside the Gardens he took the path that diverged towards the rear of the Peter Pan shrubbery. There he found a nice wooden bench giving him an excellent view, even two hundred yards away, of the path leading up from the Gardens' southern side.

Before very long, he saw the curly-headed young man, Michael, come hurrying up.

Hurry much as you like, my lad, he said to himself. Sooner you're butting up to that ladylike bit of yours, sooner I'll snatch my pic and old Butler'll give me my cash. And then... Then I'll be happy as Larry picking and choosing in the porn shop.

He waited until he was sure the two lovers would be oblivious of anything but themselves before he moved cautiously down to the corner of the shrubbery.

Yes, he thought peering round, just perfect distance, perfect light. Soon as they move a bit I'll have 'em both in perfect view. And click.

He slid back into the cover of the bushes and got his camera ready.

But when he stepped out again, camera raised, he found the lovers obstinately staying in just the position they had been in before. He lowered the camera and waited patiently. Beside him, attached to the railings, there was a small board with a long printed message attached to it. Keeping half an eye on the tableau down by the Peter Pan statue, he began to read.

## WARNING TO DOG OWNERS
### SWANS WITH CYGNETS

Last week William and Mary hatched six cygnets
at their regular nesting site on the Longwater.
William will insist on walking his brood uphill
to the Round Pond –

Suddenly he became aware of the rapid patter of dog paws coming along the asphalt path towards him.

Jesus, the St Bernard. Bloody Nana.

But during the evening before, when he was working out how to get his pic without fail next morning, he had taken the precaution of slipping into the pocket of his old black overcoat three or four lumps of sugar pinched from the bowls on the open-air tables of a café he passed. Now, quick as could be, he dipped into the pocket and held out one of them.

'Here you are, Nana girl,' he said, keeping his voice low. 'Little present for you.'

Slowly Nana approached.

Would she? Wouldn't she?

Christ, if she started that growling lark again today, he'd be finished.

But, perhaps because the dog had heard her name, she came up at last without so much as a murmur and put her soft snout into his outstretched hand. Her slobbery tongue gave him a lick. And the sugar-lump had vanished.

All right, keep her quiet. Give her another. Give her the lot, so long as down by the statue those two sooner or later feel the need to shift a bit.

But as he extracted the next lump and offered it, he saw that there had been no change in the locked embrace. Another lump, another look. Still no change.

Talk about a ruddy statue. Those two could beat bloody Peter Pan any day.

And now Nana, the world's most inefficient security guard, had realised where sugar-lumps were to be had in apparently endless profusion. She put her two heavy paws on his shoulders and gave his face, unshaven as it was, a prolonged licking.

He stood it for as long as he could. Then he gave up in disgust.

'Get down, get down, you horrible great brute.'

And, the moment he was freed from his embrace – he saw that neither Wendy nor Michael had been freed from theirs – he turned and marched away.

Another bloody wash-out, he thought. And God knows what I'll do tomorrow. But something I'll have to do. I can't not get that pic, and those books.

Next day, trusting to the lovers' routine, Old Pete was at their rendezvous well before half-past seven. Once again he had stolen a good supply of sugar-lumps. But now he had a new plan. He planted a long line of lumps at the edge of the path by the Longwater just where a dog could spot them and, with luck, no passing human would interfere. So if he heard the patter of paws coming towards him when from his cover at the corner of the shrubbery he was getting his camera into position for that vital snatch, he would throw down the three lumps he had kept in his pocket to lead the greedy beast to the start of the trail.

And if that didn't work... Well, it had got to work. The thought of those glossy mags in the porn shop was killing him.

Patiently, though not as patiently as the day before, he sat waiting on the bench at the rear of the shrubbery until he saw in the distance Michael approaching. Certain that Wendy – funny how Nana's owner and Butler Rogers's Bendy had the same name – would have already arrived in front of Peter Pan with Nana beside her almost as eager to greet young Michael as she was herself.

He sat tight and made himself count to fifty before he ventured carefully down to the corner where the day before Nana had overwhelmed him. Sure enough, peeping round, he saw the two lovers clasped tightly together. Nana, sitting there, was giving them, it seemed, an approving look. But in a moment she got to her feet and began to mosey along the path towards him.

As soon as she came within range of a low call he took his three sugar-lumps from his pocket and, with a quick 'Nana, there, girl, there', flung them further along the path. For a moment Nana ignored them, glinting though they were in the bright morning sunshine. Old Pete cursed. Would the great lumping beast come pawing all over him once again?

But, no. Suddenly she seemed to take in the first of the gleaming white lumps. She scampered towards it, put her head down, gobbled, looked up, saw another lump, scurried forward, seized it, saw another...

Christ, I've done it.

Now, now turn round a bit you silly buggers and I'll have you. Just a little bit more. Go on, girl, push him. Shove yourself up against him. Push. He'll love that. And he'll just have to take one tiny step back. Ah, now –

From somewhere not very far distant there suddenly broke into the quiet of the morning a tremendous clatter of noise. A dog's loud and furious barking and something else.

Old Pete could not stop himself just turning round to look.

Yes, by God. A big white swan, wings stretched, was strutting across the sun-dried brown grass at the foot of the wide sweep leading away to the Round Pond straight towards Nana, hissing so loudly it could be heard fifty yards away. Nana was standing her ground, barking madly, but looking as if at any moment her nerve would break. Behind the swan – it must be the William of the Warning to Dog Owners notice – six grey, fluffy, awkward cygnets looked on, undecided evidently between flight back to the lake or supportive attack.

And, of course, the noise had penetrated even into the locked lovers' aura surrounding Wendy and Michael. In an instant they broke away from each other and started off towards the fracas.

'Nana, Nana,' Wendy shouted. 'Come here, come here at once!'

'Wendy, Wendy,' young Michael shouted, as urgently. 'Don't go near. Don't go near. It's dangerous. Dangerous. Stop!'

Blackly Old Pete turned and tramped away. There wasn't going to be any pic to snatch after a business like that. Stupid woman, why couldn't she keep her damn dog on a lead as she'd been told. She must have seen that notice at the other end of the shrubbery: *Dogs must be kept on leash in this area*. Why couldn't she do what she was told?

Nevertheless next day, again well before half-past seven, Old Pete was in position once more. Nothing could go wrong this time. The day before as he had made his way cursing out of the Gardens, he had caught sight in the distance of a chastened Nana being led by the collar in a homeward direction. So no reason why there should not be a lovers' meeting again, with Nana now surely on the leash, under Peter Pan's disinterested eye. But perhaps Wendy had had to tell her husband the story of Nana's fight with the furious William? Dangerous ground there. Still, she must be clever by now at finding ways out of trouble of that sort.

53

Or she would be clever – until there landed on the old boy's breakfast table one day before much longer a stiff cardboard envelope containing a photo of herself and lover boy in this morning's body-to-body clinch.

Well, serve her right. If she wanted to do that sort of thing she ought to be ready to take the consequences. And he had to snatch that pic. The cash. He had to have it.

So he waited on the bench where he could spot young Michael before he got anywhere near the shrubbery. His camera in its old brown bag was ready as ever for instant action, film loaded, distance calculated, weather conditions – yet another bright perfect summer's morning – allowed for.

Almost at the very second that he had expected, young Michael came striding eagerly into view. Pete sat tight once again and counted to fifty, though with less slow deliberation than before. Then he went softly down to the corner and peered round, not without glancing again at the long printed screed about William and Mary and their six offspring.

What was the point of saying all that when some idiot's going to bring a dog to the Gardens without a leash? Still, little Wendy was going to have more to think about shortly than that great lolloping hound trying to get the better of a cob swan.

And, me, I'm going to have more to think about than standing here having to fight off the same great lolloping hound, or having it spoil the best chance I've yet had of getting my pic. Pic that's going to mean a happy, happy afternoon for me today shut up in my little room Victoria way, key turned in the lock, pile of mags on the bed.

Right then. And there they are, the pair o' them. Standing just at the moment and looking at each other, holding hands, with that damn dog, leash – thank goodness – tied to the bench there, sitting staring up at them both, almost as if she's a clergyman about to perform the marriage ceremony.

Marriage ceremony. Fat lot either o' them's going to worry about any marriage ceremony, I'll bet. Dirty beasts.

Aha, now they're going for it, the long lingering kiss. And, for once, just at the right angle for me. Light first class. No awkward shadows. Nothing. Hold it. Hold it just there. Lips to lips. Tongue, by the look of it, to tongue.

Kissing like that. Disgusting. Kissing. Why can't people leave all that sort of thing to the mags?

Nevertheless he raised his camera between two steady hands, put his eye to the viewfinder and there they were fairly and squarely in the frame. It was going to be a perfect pic. Perfect.

And then... Then something in the way young Michael was holding Wendy, an evident protectiveness, and something in the way she was leaning up to him as if offering him, not just that body-to-body contact, but the whole of herself, all her life, all that she was, even something in the way stupid Nana was sitting there looking at the pair of them, stump of a tail flicking to and fro on the dusty path – all combined to freeze his finger to stillness on the very point of clicking the shutter.

He wouldn't snatch his pic.

He couldn't.

Wendy's old husband would never have a stiff cardboard envelope there in front of him at his breakfast table. Wendy and Michael would go on meeting here, morning after morning. Stupid Nana would get the same walk every day, and sit waiting at the same spot whenever she got to it. Above, Peter Pan would go on and on blowing away at his silent pipe. And me, Old Pete thought, I won't get my pay from that sod Butler Rogers. I won't get the cash to go round to the porn shop. I won't spend the afternoon flipping through and through the new mags.

But – But do I actually mind? Do I mind really? Do I mind in fact if I don't never see another mag ever again?

Suppose I don't, not really. No, not really. After all, you got to grow up some time.

# TOWARDS WHAT FATE?

Every time Morgan Ransley, the poet, taking his before-breakfast walk, passed the clock tower in Kensington Gardens, the hands on each of its four faces in those days permanently saying ten to eight, he would give the face nearest him a cursory glance. So why it was he never knew, but on this particular bouncily-fine spring morning the sight of that stopped clock was suddenly the starting point for a poem. Perhaps it was because, at what is often thought of as the sober age of fifty-seven, he was head over heels in love.

But at the moment the idea entered his head, he was thinking more of his art than of his love. Nor did he have even the least inkling that from this point onwards the course of the remainder of his life was ordained.

However, just as he gave that quick glance upwards at the little decorative clock tower topping the park's ornate drinking fountain, there came into his rhyme-oriented head – his reputation had always been more for felicity of expression than for blank-verse profundity – just four limpid lines:

> Stands the park clock
> At ten to eight.
> The hands stay still,
> But life won't wait.

It was only when he was hurrying across the Bayswater Road, in the few moments allowed to pedestrians who have pressed the traffic-halting button on the lights, that a faint niggling which had gradually grown in his mind burst out in revealing light.

Of course, that bloody echo of Rupert Brooke. *Stands the church clock at ten to three/And is there honey still for tea?*

But by the time he was within a couple of hundred yards of the prosaic terrace house in Notting Hill where he had lived for all his married life he had dealt with that.

> Stopped, the park clock
> At five to eight...

All right certainly to fake – no, adjust – that time by five minutes so as to sheer yet further away from Brooke. But wrong, of course, to wrench the hour from what in fact it was. Eight it ought to be. A fellow must have some integrity.

*In the poetical home Margaret, wife of the poet, guiltily switched off the poet's word-processor. What if Morgan knew she had managed to make it work? And, oh damn, his coffee not brewed yet.*

The poet, pushing open the little metal gate of his front garden, said to himself that *eight* would be fine, too, for the rest of the poem. Because that one verse, happy *trouvaille* though it was, surely cried out for more to follow. Yes, he thought, misty though it still all is, this could prove to be something decidedly good. As telling as anything I've done for months. For years even.

And if it all came out as well as it hintingly promised, he would give it to Jen. The first poem gift he would have made her. Written in jet-black Indian ink in the fine italic hand he had so painstakingly taught himself in his younger promise-filled days. Yes, on a sheet of thickly noble paper.

While, of course, a copy would stay safely in the WP until it could go to the *Spectator,* the *Times Literary Supplement,* or *Poetry Review* in a workmanlike printed-out version.

Yes, he said to himself, inserting his key in the lock of his front door, the omens are good.

Except –

Surely there wasn't here in the hall the wonderful odour of fresh brewed coffee. Or, no, wait. Yes, there it was. Just. Margaret must have been late. Once more. And hadn't he told her again and again that any small hiccup in one's routine, if one is an artist, can wreck the whole of a day. Damn it, a poet lives on his sensibilities. One deserves the comfort of unvarying orderliness. It is necessary.

But it looked as if the coffee would be ready when he was ready for it, just as he liked it. Strong and black. After his orange juice. So all should be well. He ran upstairs to his study, booted up the WP – how he loved that expression – and typed in his first verse.

A rankling of indignation set up in his head in the Gardens next morning as, considering the day ahead, he strode past the great sweeps of upspringing orange and purple crocuses. Would he have to wait once more today while Margaret, unorganised as ever, with all the breakfast things on the table scurried to get the coffee brewing? And to the right black strength? Why could she not see to the coffee first and then, while the water bubbled through the machine, put his two egg-cups, his plate and his cup and saucer in their places. Order was not difficult to achieve. Look at the way every poem he had ever written was now there on his hard disc, filed in order of date, cross-referenced by title and first line, ready, whenever he wanted to read one of them again, to come up bright green on the screen.

But the moment on his way towards the park gate when he turned onto the path that led up to the clock tower, all irritation sank away as if a plug had been pulled from a washbasin. The poem. The sight of that roman-figure clock face would give him the next impulse. He knew it.

And there it was. Its hands still stopped at ten to – no, damn it, at five to eight. In his mind it must, must, must be five to eight.

He let himself come to a halt, something he normally prided himself on never doing while he was taking his morning exercise. If he looked at the clock face with his eyes fixed in a sort of squint, he really could – well, perhaps not absolutely – see that long minute-hand pointing to the roman XI and not to the X. Five-to, and not Brooke's blasted ten-to.

Yes, the thing would be to make each verse following that first one pick up the last line of the verse before and then add a new thought. Then in a final quatrain I'll repeat both the first two lines and add to them a really telling variation of that first thought. Thank goodness, that inner voice of mine, the poet's conscience, made me keep the fixed hour to *eight*. Plenty of rhymes for *eight*. So in the end that final verse will absolutely say what the whole of the poem is about. Meaningfully. Yes, that's what it all will be. A really meaningful thought, delightfully expressed.

That will be it.

As to what that meaningful idea will be exactly, well, the poem itself will dictate that as it unwinds in my head. Always the way to do it. Let the subconscious have its oracle say. This is going to be something really memorable. A fitting gift for Jen. Delightful, bubbling Jen. My spring queen.

No, by God, the poem will be more than just a gift. It will mark my going over to Jen, from top to toe, from head to foot. For ever.

And another verse actually came to him almost at once. Just beyond the Gardens, as he marched down the broad stretch of Palace Court, syllable after syllable fell into place with the beat of each loud footfall, the last line becoming clear as he crossed over to the big, red-brick mass of Palace Court Mansions. Given. Right. Or very nearly right. And just what I want.

> Life won't wait.
> On we must go.
> Life points the way,
> High road or low.

And this turned out to be one of the days when, as he pushed open his front door, the odour of strong black coffee warmly assailed him. Life's road, for once, not quite as low as nowadays he almost always felt that it was.

He had to run up to the study and boot up the WP fast as he could so as to get those lines down before his eggs got cold under their cosies.

Though he ought to have been reading a biography he had been sent for review, he worked on the nascent poem for most of the day. Altering a word, replacing it, altering it again. Testing each line. Saying it aloud. Savouring it.

Before he had to break off to teach his adult education class at the City Lit, another quatrain had been added to the polished and repolished previous one.

> Life won't wait.
> On we must go.
> Life paints our path,
> High road or low.
>
> High road or low,
> Some distant aim
> Is there upon a far-off day,
> A marker written with our name.

And he had felt entitled, with things coming on so well, to type in at the head of the poem the dedication, *To Jenny, with love.* Just that. A simple dignity was what was called for. Or – he scrolled back – better, *To Jenny, my spring queen, with love.* Yes, that said it. That is what Jenny is. My spring queen. The last, late, unexpected gift of my life.

At his class he was able to read out aloud the essay Jenny had submitted the week before, and to praise – a little exaggeration was surely permissible – its keen insights.

*The poet's wife switched on, located the current file, scrolled down. And there it was, what he had been so uncharacteristically secretive about, ignoring his breakfast – eggs ready, coffee blackly steaming. My spring queen. She gave a snort.*

He even went on to comment to the class on the neatness of Jenny's computer-printed text. He knew that this was going a bit far, but somehow a sudden thought of the contrast between Jen's young efficiency and disorganised, coffee-spoiling Margaret's never-abandoned 'little woman' pose – when he had first got his WP she had even said she was frightened to go near it – had pushed him into producing this irrelevant compliment. He noticed as he turned to the next class-member's work that some of them sitting there, the older ones chiefly, were looking sullenly unappreciative. Had they guessed what was going on between himself and Jen? And did he care one little bit if they had?

Next day in the Gardens, however, the sight of the clock hands still fixedly pointing to ten to eight – he had forgotten, striding up towards the drinking fountain, to close his eyes in the right squint – did nothing towards adding to the poem. Somehow what had happened at the end of his class had soured things. It had been Miss Grigston, a stout woman of much his own age, habitually dressed in a dull-green tweed suit, always ready with a depressingly crass remark when he asked for comments, who was responsible. As he had gone up to Jen when the bell sounded, he had just caught on Miss Grigston's podgy, heavy-eyebrowed face a look that might have said – no, had seemed all too clearly to say – 'No fool like an old fool.'

It wasn't true, he had kept telling himself all that evening, sitting letting Margaret's TV programmes wash over him, or just occasionally laughing at one of the jokes he happened to catch. This was something more than an old man's – no, than a middle-aged man's – absurd infatuation. This was something new in his life. A whole new direction.

He had looked across at Margaret then, her face glowingly alert to whatever ridiculous trivialities were happening on the screen. She may have guessed, half-guessed, that I am, if not having a full-blown affair, at least thinking quite a lot about some other woman. But she can have no idea what the real situation is. That I have gone over completely to Jen. Heart and soul. Or, rather, that I am on the point of doing just that.

That, when my poem is complete and I have written it out with painstaking love on my special paper, I am going to give it to my

Jenny and tell her that from that moment on we are going to share the rest of our lives.

A sharply disquieting thought manifested itself. It had been in just that way, years before, that he had written out his first love poems. The ones in *Enraptured Garland* that he had given to Margaret. *My poor Margaret. She can have no idea now how much I truly love little Jen.*

It was not only next day that the roman-numeralled clock face – still ten to eight – failed to move the poem forward. Morning after morning nothing happened. Not a whisper of inspiration. Sometimes he blamed the image of stout, unyielding Miss Grigston. Sometimes he blamed Margaret herself. For knowing about him and Jenny. For not knowing about him and Jenny. For half-knowing about him and Jenny.

But after a week, when he had taken his class once more and Jen had sat there in the front row sending her secret signals to him, in the park next morning the dam gates broke. *If clock hands once again can start...* Yes, that's how the next verse must end. A new impetus. That's what I've needed. So how will it go...?

> A marker written with our name,
> Must it be such?
> If clock hands once again
> Can start –

A rhyme. There must be one. One that will say the thought for me. *Such? Much? Clutch? Hutch?* Oh, for God's sake, this isn't a poem about rabbits. *Much? Touch? Clutch?*

No. Wait. Do it the other way round.

> A marker written with our name,
> Must such it be?
> If clock hands once again
> Can start, can't we?

Yes, yes, yes.

*Still no new verse added then. It's been days now. I wonder if... But, all the same, the bit he's done so far, with that dedication. Just like — Just like the ones he used to put on his poems for me. God, how naive he was then. How naive I was. In those days when he was courting me. Yes, that's what it was all that long ago. Courting. And now... Now what's he doing with this little bitch he's fixed his lecherous eyes on? Not courting. That's for certain. Bedding, more like. Yes, bedding her. Damn and blast the treacherous sod.*

He set off towards the big gate again, head already beginning to be filled with the beat of the lines of another verse. Yes, neat variation of the repeat line called for here.

> So can we start again
> And take a different... way? path?

Something. *And take a different...* No, I'll have to work at this. In the peace and quiet of the study. Alone. Alone with my thoughts. Of the poem. Of Jen.

He almost ran back home. Scooting across the Bayswater Road when there was a slight gap in the traffic without attempting to press the pedestrian button, pacing the length of Palace Court with ever-lengthening strides, trotting across into Hereford Road, positively darting in front of a racing early-morning truck in Westbourne Grove.

He did somehow get through his breakfast – it seemed to be one of Margaret's more organised days, though she looked a little flustered when he opened the door – but he had to abandon his second cup of coffee to thunder up to the study, slam the door behind him, boot up the WP, find the poem, zip down the lines, tap out those first words of the new verse.

> So can we start again
> And take a different...

*Road?* Yes. Yes, *road.* That was it. And *road* saying, by that sort of magic that came at times, *load.*

So can we start again
To take a newer road?
A road that's free
Of heavy load?

Yes, that's it. That is it. And for me, in real life, there's going to be that different road, that road without the heavy load I've had to carry for so many years. A road to travel along, joyously, burden-free. With my lightsome Jen.

*A newer road? A newer blasted road. I do believe he's going to… God rot him, he's thinking of leaving me. For this little bitch. Jenny Spring Queen. After all these years. After all I've done to make the bloody poet's life easy. The breakfasts always ready, the bloody odour of freshly brewed strong black coffee to greet him at the door… Then the silence in the house… And, the worst, giving up any idea of a family… All for the sake of the Muse. The bloody, bloody Muse. And now…*

It was next morning, Morgan standing still like an idiot, lightning-struck, turned to rock, in front of the ten-to-eight clock (ingeniously squinted into five-to-eight), that the last quatrain came to him. He knew he had been right to have *eight* there waiting for its clinching rhyme. The four lines were suddenly present in his head, complete. The lines that would stamp out for him, for his Jen, for the world one day, that meaning that had been there, lurking, from the very first moment.

To rhyme with *eight* only one possible word: *fate.*

Because this must be what, subconsciously, he had wanted to say from the very first. How, despite our inescapable, inherent nature, we do not have to march inexorably onwards to the one fate that awaits us.

Yes, this is what the poem has turned out to say. Despite every wrong path we might have wandered off along, even for years, for miles and miles of life's way, we can, however late, take another, newer road. The one that I shall take – I shall take today, yes, today – to my Jenny, my spring queen, my true fate.

Yes, the poem is now complete. That last verse, picking up those two first lines of all, is there for the setting down. Complete. Before the morning is over I shall have written it out from start to finish. With all possible care, on the special paper, in my beautiful italic hand that I learnt so long ago. And at the head there will be the dedication. *To Jenny, my spring queen. Now and for ever.* Make it that. And finally, I'll just put the finished version on to the WP – must arrange to have it brought round to Jenny's – to be sent in due course to whichever journal I choose for it.

> Stopped, the park clock
> At five to eight.
> The hands stay still,
> But life won't wait.
>
> Life won't wait.
> On we must go.
> Life paints our path,
> High road or low.
>
> High road or low,
> Some distant aim
> Is there upon a far-off day,
> A marker written with our name.
>
> A marker written with our name,
> Must such it be?
> If clock hands once again
> Can start, can't we?
>
> So can we start again
> To take a newer road?
> A road that's free
> Of heavy load?

Stopped, the park clock
At five to eight.
But life can lead
To some new fate.

*Some new fate… Your life lead… After all the years. After no family. After keeping the bloody house silent as the grave for the bloody Muse. For those bloody poems, written out in your bloody italic hand. Or tap-tap-tapped into your bloody computer. How I'd like to get at that last bloody poem. To Jenny blasted spring queen. And put in one of those viruses they talk about. To poison it. Kill it. And you with your break-fasts always to be there on the dot after we're back from our bloody morning walk. Coffee aroma to order. Damn and blast your two eggs, your strong coffee. Black. Strong black coffee…?*

From the *Daily Telegraph*, 24 November 1993:

# Jealous Wife Murdered Poet

Margaret Ransley was at the Central Criminal Court yesterday sentenced to life imprisonment for the murder by poisoning of her husband, the distinguished poet, Morgan Ransley, 57. Passing sentence, Mr Justice…

# SPEKE

The public parks in London open very early in the morning in summertime. But for several hours after the dawn-rising keepers have swung back the gates, the big green open spaces that are one of the chief attractions of the city remain practically deserted. One or two earnest men can be seen hurrying through to jobs that begin before most other Londoners have got out of their beds; some athletic individuals trot round in tracksuits; and a few hardy dog exercisers stand watching their pets run aimlessly about. But other than these the great parks are empty.

So it was something decidedly out of the ordinary when shortly after 5.00 a.m. one day not so long ago two contrasting figures entered Kensington Gardens, where Barrie's Peter Pan once roamed, by the gate at the southern end of its Broad Walk. One of the two was a small boy aged about six, with neatly cut fair hair above a pale face and eyes of the intensest gem-hard blue, and an overcoat of soft herringbone tweed with a neat velvet collar. He was walking very erectly and carrying a small oblong box about eight inches long by four and a half inches wide.

The girl beside him was in her early twenties and every inch proclaimed her to be that prime British institution, the Nanny. She wore a grey gabardine coat down to her knees, a grey round felt hat that matched the coat exactly, grey stockings, and neat well-polished black shoes. At ten o'clock in the morning she and the boy would have been a totally unremarkable sight coming into the park from the calmly dignified houses and apartments of Kensington. A boy and his Nanny, no more. But this was not ten: it was a little after five in the morning.

To account for the presence of Master Edward Milchester and his Nanny at that hour and in that place we must go back in time a little and consider some not uncomplicated circumstances. Edward was an only child. His father, an executive in an oil company, had by the nature of his work to be abroad a good deal. On many of these trips he took Edward's mother with him 'for the ride', as he put it, and for this reason as much as any, Edward had always had a Nanny.

His first one, who had been with him from babyhood until just after his sixth birthday, finally had to relinquish her post – a matter of varicose veins doing what the lure of sharing a sister's house at St Leonards-on-Sea had never been able to achieve. The present Nanny had been with the family only six months. This was her first job, but she was recognised to be a sensible girl and Mrs Milchester had no qualms about leaving her in sole charge of Edward when, about a week earlier, Mr Milchester had to depart for a fortnight's stay in the United States.

Mrs Milchester, of course, never quite liked leaving Edward alone with Nanny for so long, and while abroad she always spent a considerable amount of money, and often a considerable amount of time, finding Edward a homecoming present. It might be a monster penknife with eighteen different blades, or, when they went to India, a small green parakeet. (There were fearful complications about quarantine, but eventually the present had been successfully handed over.) This time Mrs Milchester intended to make the gift the very latest American toy, something over which she foresaw no difficulties.

But in the meantime Edward had become very attached to his parakeet, which, since he had been promised that before long it would be able to talk, he had named Speak. Speak, in fact, had not learned the art of conversation by as much as a single word, and perhaps it was for this reason that Edward, about two months after he had been given his pet, made a slight change in its name. He was an intelligent boy and was already able not only to read quite well but to spell with some degree of accuracy. So when one day, walking in unfamiliar parts of Kensington Gardens with his new and more athletic Nanny, he came across the simple obelisk that honours the explorer, John Hanning Speke, with its stark engraving saying *In memory of Speke. Victoria Nyanza and the Nile 1864*, he made the small alteration in the bird's name by thinking of it thereafter as Speke. The change increased, if anything, his devotion to his brilliant and beautiful but unloquacious pet.

So imagine the blank and bleak misery that settled down on him when, on the morning that his parents had been in America for just one week, he woke up to find that Speke, in his splendid antique brass cage that hung from a richly ornate stand in the window of his bedroom, was dead. Edward ate no breakfast. He ate no lunch, though Nanny herself rang Harrods and ordered the fresh myrtleberry ice cream that he'd had as a special treat on his last birthday and had frequently since extolled to her. But do what Nanny might – and she was a nice girl who hated to see anyone down in the dumps when there was anything she could do to cheer them up – say what she might, promise what she might, Edward remained inconsolable.

At about six o'clock in the evening, however, when he still had eaten nothing and Nanny was beginning to nerve herself to put through that call to America she had been tirelessly instructed she should make without hesitation 'if anything goes really wrong', the situation suddenly and almost miraculously changed.

Edward, siting on the red-cushioned window seat in his bedroom, from which he had hardly budged all day, within a few feet of the bright green corpse in its brass cage, abruptly looked up.

'He will have to be given a funeral,' he said.

Nanny, quick to sense any change of mood, seized on this possibility of a diversion.

'Oh, yes, of course,' she replied briskly. 'You can give poor Speke a really nice ceremony. And I've got just the thing that would do for a coffin.'

'What is it?' Edward asked, his voice still tear-stained but his eyes already brighter.

'It's a little wooden box that I had at Christmas. It had glacé fruits in it, and it was so strong and nice I didn't like to throw it away afterwards. But I've been wondering what to do with it.'

'Where is it?' Edward demanded.

71

'Where is it, what, Edward? Have you forgotten the magic word?'

There was a moment of flushed rebelliousness, and then Edward's normal reactions happily took over.

'Where is it, please, Nanny,' he said in rapid ritual. 'Oh, please, Nanny, where is it?'

'It's in my room. Do you want to come and fetch it?'

And in a few moments Edward had possessed himself of the plain wooden box and was eagerly discussing a suitable lining for it. But all the same there was a bright flush on his cheeks and a brilliance to his gem-blue eyes which Nanny did not altogether like.

So she insisted on him eating the rejected myrtleberry ice cream by way of supper before superintending the lining of some nice white silk inside the box, a sturdy affair about eight inches long and four and a half inches wide. Afterwards she watched over the removal of the body of the deceased, with a pair of eighteenth-century fireplace tongs from the drawing room, from where it had lain all day on the floor of the cage. But she did not see the flush disappear from the boy's cheeks, and as soon as the coffin lid had been lowered into place, she firmly ordered the young undertaker to sit down on his bed and took his temperature. It registered one whole degree above normal.

'So it's half an aspirin and bed for you, my lad,' she said.

Edward accepted the aspirin without fuss, which in itself was a little disquieting to Nanny, and allowed himself to be undressed and tucked between the sheets almost without a word. Only when he was lying flat with his fair hair spread a little on the pillow did he refer again to the subject that had made such a drama of his day.

'I've thought where the ceremony will take place,' he said.

'Oh, yes, dear. Where's that?'

'Speke will be buried under the memorial to him that stands in Kensington Gardens,' Edward declared, looking up rigidly at the ceiling high above him.

'Well, I don't think that would really be possible,' Nanny said, as she busied herself drawing the heavy red brocade drapes.

'But he must be, Nanny. He must be. You said he was to have a Christian burial. You did, you did, you did.'

'I said nothing of the sort, my lad, and well you know it. Bury him you certainly can – I'm sure we can find a corner of the garden where Daddy won't want any flowers – but he can't have a Christian burial because animals aren't Christians. They haven't got souls, you know.'

Nanny had been taught by nuns and knew her theology. But Edward was far beyond the reach of any such angels-on-the-point-of-a-needle argument.

'Animals do have souls,' he shouted back. 'They jolly well do. Or anyhow Speke did.'

Worried by his vehemence, Nanny tired to brush the matter aside.

'Well, we'll talk about that in the morning,' she said. 'You go off to sleep now and you'll feel quite different when you wake up.'

'I shall still want to bury Speke under his proper monument,' Edward replied.

'Now, we'll find somewhere lovely for him in the morning,' Nanny answered. 'But just you get it out of your head that you can go burying animals where you like in the Royal Parks.'

'But he has to be buried in a Royal Park, Nanny,' Edward explained with terrible clarity. 'His monument's in one.'

It was then that Nanny made her mistake. She was not so very experienced after all.

'Digging up the ground in the park,' she said. 'What would happen if a keeper came along?'

But she had admitted, if only remotely, the possibility. And this, to intense Edward, was the opening of a broad highway.

'We could go when there weren't any keepers about,' he began.

'There are always keepers about.'

'I bet there aren't. I bet there aren't any when the park opens at five o'clock in the morning.'

'How do you know it opens at five o'clock?'

'Because we looked at the notice board. Don't you even remember that? And it said it, five a.m. And that means in the morning. A.m. means morning and p.m. means afternoon.'

'Well, that's neither here nor there,' Nanny said, with a brisk return to the commonsense world. 'I'm not going to let you go burying that bird in the park.'

'But, Nanny, you said we could if there weren't any keepers round. And, Nanny, there won't be at five o'clock in the morning, will there? Nanny, I'm going to bury him at five o'clock tomorrow morning. I am. I am. I am. I am.'

And then Nanny saw that matters had gone too far. And adamant refusal now would mean a night without sleep. She could see it in the bright fever flush on the pale cheeks, in the sheen of sweat matting the fair hair, and above all in the glittering blue eyes.

'We'll think about the morning when we get to the morning,' she said.

For a little Edward lay there, silently claiming his victory. Nanny took a last look round. But she was not quick enough to be out of the room before a voice spoke from the bed again.

'Nanny, will you set your alarm for five o'clock? Will you? Promise?'

So she promised. And when later, after seeing that the still lightly sweating head was safely sleeping on the pillow, she went early to bed herself, worn out with the day's events, she did actually set her little travelling alarm clock for 5.00 a.m.

'Do no harm to see how he is then,' she said to herself by way of excuse.

However, long before the alarm was due to ring, an insistent tapping on her shoulder awoke her. Blearily she looked up. The pale light of earliest dawn was coming in at her open window. The hands of her little clock pointed to ten minutes to four. Edward was standing there.

'Nanny, is it five o'clock yet?'

'No, it is not, Edward. Now back you go to bed and off to sleep.'

'Yes, Nanny. But you will wake me at five, won't you?'

'All right, yes, if you promise to go to sleep now.'

'Yes, I do promise.'

And in this way it came about that the small boy in the soft herringbone tweed overcoat with the velvet collar, carrying in front of him a box measuring about eight inches by four and a half, and the girl who was obviously a British Nanny entered Kensington Gardens by the gate at the southern end of the Broad Walk shortly after five o'clock one morning.

The pair of them walked quickly up toward the deserted, wind-flecked Round Pond, followed its edge for a little until they reached a wide grassed avenue of chestnuts, and then set off along its soft turf. They had not seen a soul except one earnest-faced man carrying a red plastic shopping bag and hurrying away toward the north side of the park. Some pigeons cooed lazily from the chestnuts and, just at the start of the avenue, a big aspen sighed and sighed, like the sea rattling up the shore, as the morning breeze shook its leaves.

About halfway to the Speke memorial it became visible in the misty morning light, a pale brown spike against the green of grass and trees beyond. Edward quickened his pace.

Then when they were within fifty yards of their objective Nanny thought she saw her salvation. Round the base of the memorial a low black railing loomed.

'We won't be able to get near, Edward,' she said. 'There's a railing. I'd forgotten that.'

'I can climb over,' Edward replied, his face set and his eyes never leaving the square needle of the monument.

They reached the end of the avenue. A pigeon crossed in front of them on the asphalt path, walking with a dignified rocking waddle. Nanny saw that, in fact, the railing which consisted only of thick ornamental top and bottom bars presented no obstacle at all. She looked fearfully in all directions. No one was visible.

'Well, get on with it, and quick then,' she snapped.

Edward slipped through the railing, knelt on the border of somewhat brown grass surrounding the base of the monument itself, and placed the glacé-fruits coffin reverently down at its exact centre. Then he took from his pocket the eighteen-bladed penknife that had been another of his homecoming gifts, and with its longest and strongest blade he carved a line on the ground all round the edges of the box; then setting the box aside, he hacked away at the dried-up turf till he had removed a rectangle the size of the coffin. Next he set to work to scrabble out the powdery earth below.

Nanny, who had been watching with transfixed fascination, suddenly remembered the danger of their situation and looked wildly to either side.

'Edward,' she whispered. 'Stop! There's a man coming.'

Edward looked up from where he was squatting at his task. True enough, there was a man coming, an early-morning athlete, a short spare figure with neat grey hair, a pink complexion, and gold-rimmed glasses, wearing a royal-blue tracksuit. He was coming along the path toward them at a steady jogtrot.

Implacably Edward turned back to his digging. Nanny stood on the path a few yards away and waited, unable to move, unable to utter a word.

The regular pad-padding of the runner's sneakers was clear in the morning silence. He came on toward them at that same ominously unvarying pace. Edward dug. Nanny stood. And the runner, obliviously, passed by.

And then at last the work was done. Ceremoniously Edward lowered the little coffin into the hole. He took the grey powdery earth he had removed and dribbled it by handfuls, maddeningly slowly, on to the top of the box. He patted the crumbs down. He replaced the oblong of tangled grass that he had hacked out. Then he pronounced his funeral oration.

'Here likes Speke. He never spoke.'

To Nanny's ears the childish voice sounded clarion-loud.

But no one came hurrying up. Edward ducked under the railing and took her hand. Together they set off back, down the chestnut avenue towards the Round Pond. Only when they saw the gates at the foot of the Broad Walk again did Edward speak.

'He was a faithful pet,' he said.

It was an obituary.


Well, of course, all this is a story – fiction, make-believe, let's pretend, the purest imagination.

But, the thing is, I happened to be going through Kensington Gardens last Sunday and just by that curious spiky memorial to Speke the explorer I paused a moment to choose which path to take. And there between the railing and the base of the monument I noticed a little oblong of turf that looked deader than the surrounding grass, a papery pale patch. It measured just about eight inches by four and a half.

# RUNNERS

It was something Alicia Larmie's brother said to her once that set her off. He was on one of his rare visits to her little Kensington flat – he had some important job in television in Manchester, she had never quite understood what – and, plainly making rather desperate conversation, he had complained about the traffic on the motorway, adding 'you can tell a lot about people from the way they drive'. Mostly badly, she had understood.

But it occurred to her next day, as she entered Kensington Gardens for her early morning walk circling the Round Pond, that the same observation might well apply to the runners she saw in the park. Yes, she thought at once, that stocky woman all in blue trotting along with one of her up-and-down, up-and-down hands held in a fist: she's determined to give someone an unpleasant time before the day's out. And that young man with the headphones clamped to his ears, staring mistily at nothing: one of life's utterly self-absorbed. Or the man who passed me just as I came in, the one whose feet were going slap-slap-slap on the path with each stride: he's resigned to living set-fast in despair.

It became something of a hobby with her, this runner analysis. Almost every morning she added a new example.

The young woman prancing along in a high-cut pair of shocking pink shorts showing off the entire length of her long, long legs: not exactly there for the exercise. In contrast, the quietly trotting girl in an old pair of gym shorts and a grey top: sensible little thing who, Latin or no Latin, knew the meaning of *mens sana in corpore sano*.

Of course, Miss Larmie had never thought of running herself. She would have felt that shorts, whether bright pink or sober blue, were beneath her dignity. Not that she would ever admit, even in thought, to having a dignity to be above anything. On her annual holiday in the Lake District she wore stout jeans for hill-walking and thought nothing of it.

But she had a sharply dismissive glance for the young men in the park who seemed unable to take a morning run without kitting themselves expensively out in gleaming white trainers, shiny, multi-coloured tracksuits and, as often as not, large, much-consulted stopwatches. 'Making a production of it.' Her brother had used the phrase once, and it had stuck in her mind.

So one day when, just after she had noted, bobbing along, a young woman with a mass of blonded hair tied back with an unnecessarily large diaphanous scarlet scarf – silly: her one-word appraisal – she saw the two men in trousers and dirty tee-shirts running away in the distance, they immediately caught her attention. At once she applied herself to working out what sort of people they must be.

Clearly two of a kind. Although one was tall and heavily-built – he seemed to be the leader – and the other short and inclined to fat, as far as she could see across almost the full width of the Pond, it was plain from the curious way they were running that the two of them had very much in common. Their strides were – Miss Larmie knew this, though she could not quite say why – at the same time aggressive and... yes, surely, scared.

She actually brought her own brisk walk to a halt and stood looking at them until they disappeared among the trees down near the Albert Memorial. There was definitely something out of place about them. She had seen some curious runners in the park since she had got into this habit of noticing people's styles – the grey-head as trendily garbed as a smart young jogger: quest for eternal youth – but the two in the distance were something new. Weren't those trousers somehow too thick and heavy for running in? Their tee-shirts, even at this distance, had looked decidedly the worse for wear. And what did they have on their feet? Impossible to say definitely, far away as they were, but there was certainly no spring in their strides, nothing that bouncy running-shoes would impart. So why were they out at this early hour taking exercise? If that was indeed what they were doing.

Eventually in frustration she gave up the puzzle, in much the same way as she occasionally abandoned the *Times* crossword when the clues became too ridiculously involved. Back home to her quick breakfast and then off to work.

She would have thought no more about the two curious runners had it not been for what, next day, she read in *The Times: PIANIST FOUND MURDERED.*

And what a pianist. None other than John Breakspear. The man none of whose London concerts she had ever missed. The supreme interpreter of Brahms and Schumann.

Fiercely Miss Larmie read on down the short half-column. John Breakspear, it appeared, had been found early the day before lying dead in the front hall of his house in St Petersburgh Place, a quiet street leading up to the Bayswater Road and Kensington Gardens. A neighbour heard his doorbell insistently rung at about 7.30 a.m. Then, some five minutes later, the alarm on the outside of the house was set off and the neighbour heard a man, or two men, running down the short path to the road. The crew of a passing police car stopped for the alarm bell and then through the wide-open front door saw John Breakspear lying in the hall. As soon as they realised he was dead, with his body bearing the signs of a vicious beating, they set off to look for his attackers.

When she had read only this much, into Miss Larmie's mind came the thought of the two runners she had seen on the other side of the Round Pond the day before. She sat still and concentrated.

In her mind's eye she saw the two puzzling runners once more. There had been a plain air of exhaustion in the way they were striding out, even though they were managing to keep up a somehow aggressive unflagging pace. And, yes, the times fitted. If they were the two men John Breakspear's neighbour had heard hurrying away from his house at about 7.35, then it was quite likely that at the

Bayswater Road they had snatched at the promise of escape from the distant police car's siren offered by the open gates to the park. Almost certainly then, making their way at that peculiar run of theirs over the burnt-brown summer grass, they would have reached the place on the far side of the Round Pond where she had seen them at the time she herself was where she had been. She could fix that point on her regular perambulation of the Pond to within two exact minutes each day.

So those two were the men. The murderers.

Rapidly Miss Larmie scanned the rest of the half-column. It had been written by the *Times* crime correspondent – Miss Larmie had never been sure whether she liked that once-august journal having such a person on its staff – and so it contained a few more gleaned details of the affair. A man living at an address in St Petersburgh Mews, with the same house number as John Breakspear in St Petersburgh Place, had come forward seeking police protection. He had gambling debts and believed the pianist's attackers had intended to come to him. There was an obituary of John Breakspear on page 15.

Before she read that, Miss Larmie went round to the police station in the Earls Court Road. But it was only some weeks later that she received a request to attend an identification parade at the station in Ladbroke Grove. She intimated that the time suggested would be convenient to her and arranged to take the afternoon off from her office. She knew her duty.

She knew it, it proved when the parade took place, rather too well.

As instructed by the Identification Officer in charge of the proceedings, she walked twice along each of two lines of nine men put in front of her in a big, bare room smelling of the floating dust from recent hasty sweeping. Each line, it had been explained to her, contained one of the two suspects who had eventually been arrested as known 'heavies' from the criminal fringe of the gambling world. She looked man by man at the silently staring faces. She moved her glance from head to foot up and down each of them, and then down to the number chalked on the floor in front.

And she could not in conscience tell herself that any of the men there were the two runners she had seen that summer's morning making their way in such a distinctive manner towards the gates of Kensington Gardens near the Albert Memorial.

'No,' she said at last. 'No, I cannot really recognise either man.'

'You do realise, madam,' the Identification Officer said, plainly attempting to conceal a feeling of frustration, 'that you are the only witness we have been able to find who can place the two of them at that location at the time in question.'

'No. No, I was not aware of that.'

The Identification Officer gave a little cough.

'I won't in any way press you, madam,' he said, 'to agree to anything against your better judgement. But can I urge you to look at these men once again?'

Miss Larmie thought for a few moments.

'No, Inspector,' she said eventually. 'I have given all the men a most thorough scrutiny, and I cannot say, I cannot say with certainty, I cannot truthfully say at all, that any of them are those men I saw running in the park that morning.'

'Very well, madam. If that's your final...'

'No. Stop.'

'Yes? You'll have another try?'

'Well, I will. Under certain conditions.'

'Conditions? I'm not sure we can agree to any conditions. Parades such as this are conducted according to a strict code of practice.'

'So it would not be possible for me to see these men running?'

'Running? To see them running?'

'Yes. You understand, that is how I did see them – if it was them I saw – that morning. And, as it so happens I am rather – well, rather a connoisseur of runners.'

She regarded with equanimity the look of *Jesus, not another one* she had received.

'Perhaps I should explain. I walk in Kensington Gardens every morning. At a time when there are usually a number of runners there. And I have made a certain study of them, of their way of running, of what that tells one about them. And so when I saw those two men running there that morning, I paid particular attention to the way in which they ran. And I think it's possible – only possible, mind – that if I saw all these men actually running I would be able to pick out with some degree of certainty the two I saw at that time.'

The *Jesus, not another* look had faded away.

'Well, madam, under the code by which we operate you are permitted to request the members of the parade to move. But – But I'm not sure whether that would extend to running. How – er – far would you want to see them go?'

'Oh, for at least twenty yards. I would need to be able to assess their style.'

'Their style?'

'Yes. Yes, inspector, it was their style of running that drew my attention to those two men in the park. Their style.'

'I see. Well. Well, I shall have to take advice. Yes, advice. Would you mind waiting for a little?'

'Not at all.'

So, nearly an hour later two lots of nine men, each now with a sheet of paper tied round his chest with a boldly inked number on it, guarded by half-a-dozen studiously indifferent constables, ran in turn at a steady pace from one corner of the car park behind the station across to the opposite one.

And after the first lot had completed the course, Miss Larmie said 'Number Four', and after the second lot had done, she said 'Number Six'.

Then the Identification Officer was unable to restrain a small, tight smile of satisfaction.

Months went by. At last Miss Larmie received notification from the Crown Prosecution Service that she was required as a witness at the Central Criminal Courts on a date in April. She wrote acknowledging the letter and said she would be there.

The morning of the day of the trial was a particularly fine one. Miss Larmie entered Kensington Gardens at her customary hour with perhaps a little more spring in her step than usual. She even conceded that the glittering gilding on the tall black railings of Kensington Palace – why did they also need a policeman standing guard inside among all the flowerbeds? – which on most mornings, as she passed by, she condemned as decidedly too showy, gave in the bright sunlight an extra sparkle to the day.

She wondered if she might see a new runner to add to her by now large collection. And just as she was doing so, she heard coming up behind her the loud steps of a running man. She decided not to turn her head to see him, but to try from the sound of his feet alone to make a judgement about him.

Yes, to begin with, the man's steps – she had no doubt from the loudness of them that it was indeed a man coming up quite fast – indicated, surely, someone new to the business of Kensington Gardens running. Their thudding lacked any of the assured regularity of the daily runner. But, yes, though heavy the steps were determined rather than downcast, not at all like the slap-slap-slaps of the man she had long ago analysed as being set-fast in despair. So, a newcomer. And one, yes surely, lacking any sort of sensitivity. Someone, too, who would be determined to gain –

The heavy thudding runner overtook her.

Yes, certainly a newcomer. Even wearing, this early in the morning, a leather jacket, heavy jeans and ordinary shoes. A good puzzle here.

And then, instead of thundering on beside the Round Pond, the man abruptly halted and swung round.

'Want a word wiv you,' he said to Miss Larmie.

'With me? I think there must be some mistake.'

The man sent a great puff of heavy, exhausted, ill-smelling breath out on to Miss Larmie's face.

'Yeah,' he said. 'Mistake. That's what there 'as bin. Your mistake, Miss Alice Larmie.'

'Alicia,' Miss Larmie corrected sharply. Being given the wrong forename was something she particularly objected to.

'Never mind what you call yerself,' the man answered, still blocking her way with his broad, swagger-bellied body. 'I got something ter tell you. That mistake. The one you made.'

'I don't understand a single thing you are saying. Will you please get out of my path.'

'What I'm saying is: you made a mistake when you identified two friends of mine back here in Kensington Gardens last summer. A mistake. Unnerstand?'

'I certainly do not understand. I very much doubt if you should be speaking to me about your friends at all. But, let me tell you, I certainly did not make any mistake when I identified them as being here in Kensington Gardens at the time I said they were.'

The man looked down at her.

Another puff of foul exhausted air.

'But you're going ter say you made a mistake. At the trial at the Bailey today. You're going ter say you got it all wrong. They was never nowhere near 'ere at all.'

'I most certainly am going to say nothing of the kind. I made no mistake, and when I am asked I shall simply tell the truth.'

'I wouldn't, not if I was you.'

'But you are not me. I strongly suspect you very seldom tell the truth, whereas I am accustomed to do just that.'

'That's enough o' your lip. Now, get this. You'll say at the Bailey you never saw my mates that time, or it'll be the worse for you.'

He looked at her. As if she was a baffling piece of apparatus, a video that needed its time-clock changing.

'You know as 'ow they went round ter –' he said, before coming to a bewildered halt. 'Well, it's like this, see. You know as 'ow they meant ter go round to 'im, feller as wouldn't pay up. Only they got the address a bit wrong. Well, if you don't want what ought ter 'ave 'appened to that feller ter 'appen ter you termorrer, just do what you're told, orright? Stand up there in the box an' say you made a mistake. Anyone can make a mistake. An' you did.'

With that the big man brushed past Miss Larmie and set off back towards the entrance to the Gardens she had come in at herself. Still at his awkward heavy run.

After she had given her evidence at the Central Criminal Court that afternoon, and had dealt calmly with defending counsel's insinuations as to her reliability, Miss Larmie did think to seek out a police officer and tell him about the man who had spoken to her.

'Yes,' he said, soothingly, 'we do get threats of that nature from time to time. As a general rule that's all they amount to, threats. But I'll get in touch with your local station and arrange some protection, just in case.'

Next morning, stepping out of the mansion block at her customary 7 a.m., Miss Larmie felt a twinge of shame when she saw that there was a bored-looking constable standing on the pavement there. She crossed the High Street and walked, a little more quickly than usual, up Church Street to the path that led to the entrance to the park beside Kensington Palace.

When she passed the spot where the big man with the unpleasant breath had accosted her, she gave a little shudder and mended her pace once again. But her circuit of the Round Pond awaited.

It was when she was about halfway round, just by the little wooden shed where a small boat is kept for emergency use, that it happened. Out from the far side of the shed came her tormentor of the day before, and in his hand there was a nasty-looking, thick, little cosh.

Miss Larmie did not hesitate. The man was still two or three yards away. She wheeled round and took to her heels. And heard at once on the tarmac of the wide path round the Pond the thud of heavy feet behind her.

For half a minute or so she ran blindly forwards. Anything to get away from that bulky, cosh-wielding figure. Then she began to think. So far, it seemed, she had been able to keep far enough ahead. It was plain from the day before that the man behind was hardly in training, while she herself, toughened by hard walking up the Lake District fells, was always in excellent condition.

But, if the man was really determined, he might be able to put on a desperate spurt and catch her. He was tall. His legs must be a good deal longer than her own.

And there was nobody about. There seldom was on this side of the Pond at this early hour. She could shout, while she still had the breath. But it was by no means certain that any of the runners plodding or steaming along the Broad Walk away at the other side of the

Pond would hear her. Or take any notice of they did. She knew all about the impenetrable aura runners were apt to wrap themselves in.

So nothing for it but to do what she could to put as much distance as possible between herself and the man with the cosh.

Until...

She set herself a good steady fast pace. Behind she could hear the thud of pursuing feet. But the occasional grunts of effort that had come to her ears at the beginning of the chase seemed no longer to be audible. She hoped this meant she was far enough ahead. She did not dare slow her run by glancing back to see, even for a moment.

They rounded the Pond. Still no one particularly near. Only a single runner, a young enough man, heading up the Broad Walk away towards the Elfin Oak at the other end of the Gardens. And, even at a distance, she could see the earphones clamped to his head. Another Mr Self-absorbed.

No, nothing for it but to hope her plan would work.

Now, reaching the strip of browned grass between the Pond and the Broad Walk, she did dare for one instant to glance back. When the sound of heavy steps on tarmac was no longer there she would not know what the situation was. She saw now that as a runner she was in distinctly better shape than the big man. He was now more than ten yards behind.

Too much?

She forced herself to slacken her pace, and, when her pursuer reached the Broad Walk and his steps could be heard again on the hard surface, she guessed he was now a yard or two closer.

On she ran. Down the incline beyond the Broad Walk, and onwards. And then, yes. She flung herself against the tall railings of the palace and called out, with all the remaining breath in her lungs, to the policeman still there on the far side.

'Officer, this man is threatening me.'

The big man came to a halt, gasping for air. He was just six or seven yards away. He looked at her. He looked at the high railings with their glittering gilt tops. He looked at the policeman guarding the royal personages within.

The policeman pulled a radio from his belt.

The big man wheeled round, dropped the little cosh he had not ceased to grasp and shot off, though at a wretched lumbering pace.

'I think you should say on your radio, Officer, that he's making for the Queen's Gate,' Miss Larmie called out, breathing back to normal.

It was well into the autumn when Miss Larmie received another notification to attend the Central Criminal Court where a man, identified from his sweaty fingerprints on the cosh he had dropped, was to be tried for committing Affray under the Public Order Act 1986.

She attended, gave her evidence in an admirably concise manner and saw her would-be assailant sent to prison. But after this, in the mornings in Kensington Gardens, she no longer attempted to analyse the personalities of the runners who plodded or skimmed, pelted or bowled along, darted past or trotted by.

# MR IDD

Mr Idd came into my life one Sunday afternoon in Kensington Gardens. It was a chilly day in early Spring with a sharp easterly wind, although bright sunshine had tempted a good many walkers to stride out along the Broad Walk. Mr Idd was one of them.

Of course Mr Idd was not his real name. How should I know what a total stranger called himself? But, as you will see, 'Mr Idd' was a good label to attach to him, and I bestowed it unconsciously the moment I became fully aware of him. The moment he did that extraordinary thing. The first of many.

Freud may be somewhat discredited nowadays. But all the same his great simplification of the human psyche into workaday Ego, sternly controlling Superego and anarchic, pleasure-first Id still seems to me a model that helps to explain our often wonderfully strange goings-on. And my own extraordinary experiences with the man I at once at that first encounter named Mr Idd surely bear this out.

Not that what happened was, in itself, utterly extraordinary. You might with reason have described it as no more than a piece of spontaneous fun. But by the standards of anything like normal behaviour on a Sunday afternoon in sedate Kensington Gardens it was certainly more than a little eccentric.

What happened was this. I was marching along the Broad Walk myself, breathing in the fresh chill air, feeling quite pleased with life. Mr Idd must have been almost beside me going in the same direction. Not that I had any idea at the time who it was who for the past several minutes must have been seeing the same odd spectacle a little way ahead of myself, a man dressed, heaven knows why, from head to foot as a parody of the great detective, Sherlock Holmes. Deerstalker hat, Inverness cape, and even, just visible when he chanced to turn his head, curved pipe in mouth. Altogether an eye-catching sight, if a ridiculous one. The fellow was not exactly hurrying, sneaking looks round all the time in fact, as if secretly hoping to catch glances of approbation. And I remember thinking how it would pay him out if I were to overtake him, turn and sharply greet him face to face as Holmes.

It was Mr Idd who did just exactly that. He marched briskly forward until he had just gone past the fellow, and then, turning abruptly, he confronted him with the immortal words Irene Adler called out in the story 'A Scandal in Bohemia'.

'Good-night, Mr Sherlock Holmes.'

It was a highly comical moment. The Holmes lookalike, though he evidently had been seeking admiration or at least covert recognition, was absolutely put out to have his get-up acknowledged in this blatant fashion.

He stopped in his tracks. His mouth opened, and the famous drooping pipe fell with a little clatter to the ground. He even produced some sort of sound, though what he was trying to say, if he even knew himself, came out as no more than a choked gurgle.

I stood there looking, and by the time the Holmes figure had recovered his wits, scrabbled up the pipe and stalked furiously away, Mr Idd had vanished

I might perhaps never have thought of the incident again, comical though it was – inwardly I giggled over it long after – except that within a week there was Mr Idd once more. It was in the West End, though I suppose it is not really very surprising to encounter there more than once any one of the many people who have occasion to be in what is after all quite a small area, a mere square mile or so.

What Mr Idd did this time, however, was a whole step further removed from normal conduct. Once again, it seemed, we had been walking along side by side, almost together. This time, though, it was in the morning, and we were going down St James's Street towards Pall Mall where I was to lunch at one of the clubs. Ahead of us, in much the same way as the Holmes *doppelgänger* had been a week earlier, there was striding a more-than-typical businessman. Black jacket, striped trousers, rolled-to-needle-thinness umbrella and, crowning the whole, a particularly well-brushed bowler hat worn aggressively tilted forward. He was carrying himself very upright, and even from behind he looked infuriatingly self-confident.

For a little I watched him making his way along nine or ten yards in front of me, swinging slightly that rolled umbrella, and I wondered whether anything would ever knock him off his perch.

Mr Idd showed me what would. From somewhere close to me he quickened his pace, caught up with the stiffly correct figure ahead and simply reached over and lifted the bowler off his head. For a few swift paces he marched onwards carrying his trophy. Then, placing it with immense care on the roof of a car parked beside the pavement, he strode off.

I had not recovered from my astonishment – nor had the abruptly deflated businessman – before Mr Idd disappeared. But now he was firmly established in my mind, name and all, and I felt certain that, somewhere, at some time, I was going to see him again.

Several months passed, however, before he manifested himself. But then it was in an altogether more disconcerting way.

It was not, this time, in that part of London where, because so many places of business and entertainment are concentrated, you are not surprised to see almost anyone you know. It was actually in the pleasant, mildly prosperous part of Notting Hill where I live myself.

A few discreet yards off bustling Westbourne Grove there is a shop – no, establishment is the right word – that offers to the trendy, and well-padded, a variety of luxury bathroom fittings. Its window is usually made over as a mock-up of the sort of bathroom its clientèle is expected to have. There is often a long, deep tub with taps that at least look as if they are gold plated. Beside it, artfully scattered on the tiled flooring, there will be an assortment of toilet preparations bearing exotic names. Sometimes the window is given over to a whole collection, tub, basin, toilet and bidet, all decorated in the same prettified pattern, little multicoloured flowers or perhaps a ceramic spread of bright green ferns.

To tell the truth, the whole place gets under my skin. I would never think of replacing the plain white tub and basin in my own flat with any of its products. 'Pretentious' is the word that comes to my mind each time I pass by. Yet I must admit that, if I do not exactly linger in front of its wide plate-glass window, I do almost always glance in. If only to see how far they have gone this time in the way of up-to-the-minute fancy décor.

But imagine my feelings one day, having thought as I turned the corner that the exhibits had been renewed, when there in the window, in full view of anybody in the street, was Mr Idd. He had marched up to the toilet bowl of the display – its smart wooden seat, I saw, was painted to look like marble – and, turning now, he dropped his trousers and sat.

Can he really be going to –

But before he did, if that was his intention, two of the shop's staff came pushing through the narrow entrance at the rear of the window area, seized him, one by either arm, and hauled him to his feet. I foresaw then, in a moment of chill realisation which swept away the inward laughter bubbling through me, the arrival of the police. Mr Idd would be given in charge. There would be a court appearance. Perhaps detention as being of unsound mind.

None of that happened. Mr Idd simply reached down, hauled up his trousers and, with what might be thought of as superhuman strength, flung the two staff members aside and strode out. Disappeared.

Soon I even began to wonder if the incident had happened at all.

But the thought of it left my mind awash with conflicting feelings. On the one hand I could not help admiring Mr Idd for his daring. Yet doing what he had threatened to do – would he really have gone as far as the ultimate defilement, I asked myself – was something more than unsettling to think about. Mr Idd, I decided, was not a person I wanted ever to encounter again.

And I had a disquieting feeling that somehow I had not seen the last of him. By any means.

Yet it was, again, several weeks before he materialised once more. This time it was not even in London. I was, as it happened, up in Birmingham for a meeting. It ended sooner than I expected, and I found myself at a loose end in that unfamiliar city, waiting till it was time for my train back. I was wandering about, unable to make up my mind whether to go for a drink I did not particularly want or to find the Art Museum and spend a few minutes there – too few, no doubt, to be worthwhile – or simply to stroll about absorbing the atmosphere, such as it was.

Then I saw him.

He was, of course, immediately recognisable although, as I said, it had been weeks since I had sight of him trousers down in that shop window, and months since I was a hapless witness of those two more innocent incidents. This time, instead of apparently walking along somewhere just behind or beside me, I became aware of him a short distance ahead. I was making my way aimlessly along a greasy narrow pavement bordering a wide sweep of comparatively deserted roadway. I have no idea what the short street is called, or even exactly where in Birmingham it is, except that it cannot be far from the centre. It links two much busier streets, and traffic along it is sparse, although the vehicles that use it go at a fair speed.

I took in the presence of Mr Idd just after I noticed a blind man waiting to cross at the pavement's edge, waving his white stick in a manner that struck me as more than a little peremptory. With that sharpness of hearing the blind develop, he must have detected approaching footsteps above the unending grumble of the nearby traffic because he turned and directly requested – no, demanded – assistance.

And in answer Mr Idd did an altogether extraordinary thing. Even a terrible thing. Instead of taking the man's arm and, after looking to left and right, seeing him across the wide roadway, or instead even of ignoring the brusque request – I remember thinking how some disabled people seem to feel they have almost seigneurial rights over others – he simply stopped just behind the fellow and snarled at him.

'Don't be so damned helpless. If you want to cross, cross.'

Whether he then gave him a little push, or whether the blind man was so startled that he unthinkingly set off without listening for any oncoming vehicle, I have never been able to decide. But set off he did. Unhesitatingly, on to the wide expanse of tarmac.

I stood where I was.

Was a car going to come zooming round and be unable to avoid the sudden, unexpected figure making his way over to the far side, white stick waving like the pointer of an out-of-kilter metronome? If anything came round the bend, it was almost certainly not going to have time to take avoiding action.

My heart was, as they say, in my mouth. And yet, I must admit, as the same time I experienced a tiny, subterranean whickering of pure excitement. Much as if I was watching some dangerous sporting event on television, and knew it was all right to seem callous because if anything too appalling happened it would be edited out. But the excitement was still there, despite the blind man's wavering progress being no TV recording.

In fact, the car that did come speeding round did not actually touch him. It must have skimmed his coat-tails, though, before it whirled on, horn furiously hooting.

So no real harm done. But there I was, left with the horrible suspicion – or more than suspicion, somehow a certain knowledge – that the next time I encountered Mr Idd what he would do would be yet more unthinkable.

I came to dread the day. It became an obsession with me. I knew – though I was aware, too, that rationally I could not know – that sooner or later I would see Mr Idd at work again. And that, when I did, something a whole stage worse than the incident with the blind man was going to take place.

Before long I could scarcely think of anything else. The least circumstance would cause that irrational fear to bubble to the surface of my mind – the sight of a blind person's white stick, an advertisement making use of the Sherlock Holmes deerstalker and curved pipe image, each and every time I happened to see a bowler hat on some smart City gent. Anything remotely connected with Mr Idd would set my fears spiralling upwards.

My work began to suffer, quite seriously. I would be busy reading the journals it was my task to keep abreast of, and by chance come across a single word that would trigger me off – *pipe, umbrella, bath.* Even one of my colleagues saying 'Good-night' as we left in the evening would connect in a single jagged instant with the impish desire I once had to confront that comical man in Kensington Gardens, and I would hear again the words 'Good-night, Mr Sherlock Holmes', which Mr Idd had, as it were, pronounced to him for me.

Soon I even found I could no longer bear to set foot in any part of St James's Street. I would go almost any distance to reach a destination I could have got to in ten minutes by the direct route. It was not that I feared seeing Mr Idd where I had seen him before; it was that anywhere in the whole street might cause me just to think about him. To wonder in dread when he would make his reappearance.

Worst of all, perhaps, I developed an aversion to using the lavatory. A phobia. Each time I needed to go to it I would see in my mind's eye Mr Idd dropping his trousers in that shop window, and my natural functions would clam up inside me. I had to have recourse to the most violent aperients, and soon came to exist in a state of constant physical misery.

Eventually I decided to take a fortnight's leave in a final effort to break the invisible grip. I went to Paris. Perhaps, I thought, completely different sights and sounds would get the nonsense out of my head. I would cut myself off from every familiar sight. Speak, read, think if I could, in a wholly different language. Surely then I would rid myself of the ever-nudging thought of Mr Idd.

But I was mistaken. It was in Paris that I saw Mr Idd once more.

I was in the Louvre, looking at Leonardo's *Mona Lisa*. After many years' absence I was seeking once again to get straight in my mind just what that enigmatic face had to say about the human personality, asking myself whether the great lady from the far past was smiling with gentle love or with the tinge of hostile contempt that I had sometimes felt emanated from her. Or, rather, I was attempting to do that. The crowd in front was, as always, impossibly dense. There must have been at least thirty people craning and jostling to get their glimpse, most of them of course altogether ignoring every other wonderful work of art in the museum with, I suppose, the exception of the Venus de Milo. I remember as I stood at the outer edge of the mob – no other word – that there came into my mind a travel article about Paris I had seen in some colour supplement in which the writer had happily claimed all that you needed in order to 'do' the Louvre was fifteen minutes to cross off those two masterpieces.

But at last I managed to get near enough, right up to the rope keeping sticky prying fingers away, to be able to see the picture whole. And it was just as I began to let flow into me that calm, if ambiguous, statement Leonardo put on canvas all those years ago that, first, I heard a twangy American voice proclaim, just to show she knew what had to be appreciated in the world-famed painting, 'Gee, what an antique smile', and, next, I was aware between myself and the picture of a blotting-out, dull, black form I somehow knew at once was Mr Idd. Then, immediately, there came a terrible, sharp rending sound.

The next moment Mr Idd was no longer there. Where he had gone, how he had dissolved among that thickly crowding mass of onlookers, I could not say. But he had vanished. And the *Mona Lisa* was ripped from top to bottom.

You must remember, even though it was a good while ago, the sensation that act of desecration caused. What I remember, however, is quite another feeling. I found – try as I might to dissociate myself from it – that I was sharing with Mr Idd what I can only call a sense of holy joy at the sheer daring of the thing he had done. At its defiance. At the magnificent snook it cocked at all those gawpers and gapers.

And that made me fear more than ever the day when once again Mr Idd would be there. As I knew he would be. Knew with utter inevitability.

You will almost certainly have remembered that attack on the *Mona Lisa*, even though restoration work has long since obliterated every sign of it. What you may not remember, though it came not long afterwards, was the attack made on Sir Elton Dugbury

You may not even remember Sir Elton. He was not, after all, a very important figure in the national life of Great Britain, even though he was a colourful personality who bounced and bullied his way over the years into several minor ministerial appointments. Outspoken if nothing else, and crudely photogenic with the embroidered waistcoats he chose to wear, he frequently figured in the headlines. There was his remark, made at the height of the Cold War, that none of the trouble need have occurred if both the Russians and the Americans had been taught to play cricket. Then there was the time he said there would be many fewer cases of rape if women would only learn to keep their legs together. And once he stated that there was nothing wrong with the arts that cutting off subsidies for everything except the Covent Garden opera wouldn't cure.

That off-the-cuff insult came shortly before Sir Elton was attacked. In the very Lobby of the House of Commons. I was there myself taking part in a protest, so angry – my work is in the field of the arts – that all my dread of encountering again the bogey that had come to haunt me had been chased for once from my head.

Sir Elton's contemptuous words – he was a junior Treasury minister at the time and might have had some responsibility for allocating arts funds – seemed to epitomise everything I thought wrong with the ruling classes in Britain. Their insensitivity, that swaggering belief in whatever happened to come into their heads, any feeling for the finer things manifesting itself only when, like opera, they cost a great deal of money. What happened was that Sir Elton, either not realising the demonstration was taking place or, perhaps more likely, delighting in brazening it out, came down to the Lobby just when it was at its height. There was an immediate chorus of booing. Sir Elton – he certainly did not lack courage, whatever else was missing from his make-up – promptly got back on the steps leading into the Lobby and trumpeted out something about 'long-haired intellectuals'. It was difficult to hear exactly what. But the defiant shout sent a wave of angry protesters converging on him. I was among them myself, swept along whether I wanted to be or not.

And then the attack happened. A moment before I had become aware – emotions at once battered me back and forth – of a terribly familiar sight. There, in the front of the crowd sweeping towards the provocative figure in the pink-flowered waistcoat, was Mr Idd.

How he had managed to smuggle a handgun through the security checks was something that caused a flurry of questions afterwards. But smuggled in it was, and within three or four feet of that flowered waistcoat it was fired.

But this time Mr Idd was unable to vanish in the way he had that Spring afternoon in Kensington Gardens, or later in St James's Street, or from that bathroom shop with the pretty-pretty toilet bowl in its window, or even after he had desecrated the *Mona Lisa* itself.

No, this time he was caught.

He is in prison now. Broadmoor. The institution for the criminally insane. He is still his old self, despite such treatment as they give him. For long periods he is altogether quiescent, and then he breaks out. He plays some trick on one of the officers. Suddenly spitting in his face. Or pretending to be dead. There is not a lot he can do, but he is determined not to be totally suppressed.

You will ask how I know this. It is because, of course, I can still watch him.

But you must – you must – believe me when I say that all along I did truly see him as someone else. As someone I was able to observe from, as it were, a short distance away. You must believe that. You must.

# PHYSICAL ENERGY

There can be very few people who have not at one time or another eaten, even if they would be inclined to deny it, a Merry Bar. Not at all classy but alluringly sweet and biscuity with, on their deeply chocolate-brown wrappers, that small silver image of a high-prancing horse, they were invented – a fact perhaps almost forgotten now – in the late 1940s by one Herbert Merridew. And, thanks to the dynamic energy with which he marketed them, never slackening until his retirement, they made him his huge fortune.

So it should not be surprising that in the last years of the twentieth century Herbert Merridew himself, bent with age, crippled by arthritis but with eyes bird-sharp and acquisitive as ever, should leave his comfortable ground-floor flat in the Bayswater Road every morning to walk, slowly as a neck-swivelling tortoise, across to Kensington Gardens. There he would go all the way down the long straight path that leads from the Inverness Gate to where G.F. Watts's magnificent bronze statue of a horse and its far-gazing rider, Physical Energy, stands high on its granite plinth. Because it is the outline representation of that statue that is silver-printed on each and every Merry Bar. And – something Herbert Merridew had never confided to anybody – it was the statue itself that gave him his initial impulse to transform the moribund sweet-making firm he had inherited, churning out day by day its small quotas of humbugs, lollipops and pear-drops, into the original manufactory of the Merry Bar.

A newcomer to London, he had been wandering one Sunday in a fairly dispirited way through the Gardens when, looking up, he saw Watts's statue. Immediately it enthralled him. The energy of that huge horse, forefoot uplifted to trample under its huge hoof everything in its way, seemed to enter into his innermost being. The held poise of the rider, back-leaning, tensed to the utmost for his steed's forward leap, sent a thrilling echo through and through him. Even the vigour with which the sculptor had scooped out each half-inch of horse flesh and rider's muscle infused him with an immediate and palpitating energy of his own. Hardly a minute had passed before he had turned abruptly on his heel, raced with ever-lengthening strides back to his modest Bayswater rooms, flung himself indoors, seized paper and pencil, and with swift, thick lines brought to life what had until then been only the vaguest of ideas in the back of his mind. There in a quarter of an hour or less was the shape and plan of that irresistible chocolate-and-biscuit sweet that was before long to sweep into its maw the whole of postwar, austerity-ridden Britain and eventually to triumph over the entire known world.

But to eighty-six-year-old Herbert Merridew, as he painfully made his way along the path one morning, all that seemed infinitely far away. Now the thought that, as often as not, filled his mind during his daily self-set period of exercise was deciding exactly where it was that he was going to die. At which precise spot. He felt he was like a kitten-heavy mother cat looking here, there and everywhere for the right place to give birth to her litter. He knew – there was nothing wrong with his mental faculties, however dimmed his physical ones – that he really had no choice in deciding on the spot where he would, not give birth, but simply give up life. When at last there came his heart's final dulled beat he would be wherever he happened to have got himself to at that vital muscle's chosen moment.

But nevertheless he liked to toy with the thought of just where that might be. Sometimes he chose somewhere nicely incongruous. Say if, feeling more than usually unwell setting out for his daily pilgrimage to Physical Energy, he had stopped to rest in one of the phone boxes just beside the park gate. Then he would be found dead, still perhaps upright, apparently gazing at all the prostitutes' cards he, sharp-eyed as ever, had in recent years noticed stuck up there. There would be a certain rightness about that, he reflected with a sudden sharp smile. In his day the energy he had happily possessed from the moment he had conceived the notion of the Merry Bar had led him into countless on-the-side sexual adventures. But on the other hand, he might just come to his end one night safe in his own respectable bed.

Or would he die with a Merry Bar – he was still sent the regular supply he had insisted on twenty years before when he retired – half-eaten in his mouth? Or, a nicely ironic end, with a half-chewed bar of one of a rival firm's products? After all, sometimes he sent his man, Pellet, out to buy one or other of them, little though that desperately correct fellow liked the task. And how earnestly had Pellet begged, just yesterday, to be allowed to accompany him on his walk. How tactfully the poor fellow had edged on to the subject of his infirmities. But he had been unyielding. No, although any day his outing might be his last, he wanted to be able to set off at whatever hour he could no longer bear to lie sleepless in bed. As soon as it was light, or at eight, or nine or ten. Whenever. Pellet was to lay out his clothes the night before and leave him to work his way into them at his leisure and as his *difficulties* – yes, that was the word Pellet had found – permitted.

So this morning it was not yet half-past six when he set out, sturdy walking-stick in hand, across the wide stretch of the Bayswater Road. No traffic, thank goodness. So nothing to complicate his step-by-step progress from one kerb to the other. And no one about either to give a pitying, contemptuous thought to the aged, bent old man off to make his way down the long path to where, no longer clearly to be seen with his dimmed sight, Physical Energy awaited.

Now that would be an appropriate place to come to the end. No one, in fact, likely to know just how appropriate. But the little secret would give him, were he to know afterwards what went on happening in the world, a pleasing extra of irony. Dying somewhere which ought to give the newspapers a nice peg to hang his millionaire's obituary on, and no one realising it.

Or would someone as bright and as sharp as he once was himself remember what precisely the hardly-ever-looked-at little horse-and-rider on the Merry Bar depicted? Probably not. Who delighted in Watts's statue nowadays? Only the children who paid tribute to it in clambering up its sides.

But, wait. There was someone about at this early hour.

A girl was standing leaning listlessly up against the wall under the park railings a few yards along on the other side of the gate from the phone boxes. She was, he saw looking more carefully, a drab sort of creature. Not well dressed. Black cotton skirt down at one side and her purple jacket half off one shoulder and bunched up on the other. She was looking vaguely towards Notting Hill Gate, and he wondered what on earth she was doing there as early in the day as this.

Then, suddenly, he knew. She must be a streetwalker.

He remembered now that a dozen years or more before he had once, somewhat to his surprise, been accosted in the Bayswater Road at much the same early hour and, as much because of the unlikeliness of the encounter as anything, had abruptly felt willing to begin his day in the way he had often ended it. This girl, despite her lack of interest in her surroundings, must be another one such, hoping for a little-likely customer.

Almost without realising it he straightened his back, lifted up his head, swung his stick jauntily as if it was not pretty well a necessity but simply a dandy's accoutrement. And in half the time it generally took him, he reached the far side of the wide road. Not that he had any intention... But no harm in not appearing utterly decrepit, if the girl happened to glance at this oldish fellow making his way into the Gardens.

As she was doing now.

And on her pale, unprepossessing face – smudged lipstick, hair in a mess – there came, he saw, a hinted look of speculation.

'Good morning,' he said, feeling a dart of pity for the spiritless-looking creature trying at this unlikely hour to make herself a few pounds.

He saw she was now looking at him more sharply.

'D'you want business?'

Well, he did not. Those days were gone. Far gone. But it would be amusing to talk to the creature for a minute or two, and perhaps he could cheer her up a bit. She looked as if she needed all the lift anything or anybody could give her.

'You're out very early,' he said.

She was still looking at him with evident wariness. But, hopefully, she answered.

'Did no good last night. Thought I'd better give it a try this morning. What yer got in mind then?'

He shook his head sadly.

'My dear, at my age it is all in the mind, I'm afraid. In the mind and nowhere else. But, listen, let me give you something. If only in remembrance of many past occasions.'

Not without a wince of pain he put a hand into his inner pocket and tugged out his wallet. Glancing up he saw the look of greed that had appeared all over her pallid, worn, early-morning face.

Ah well, he thought, I suppose the most that a sparkless creature like this one can rise to, confronted by the ruin of a man I am, is to hope to satisfy her greed.

He opened the wallet and saw that there was, happily, a five-pound note sticking up, conveniently easy to grasp between not wholly reliable arthritic fingers. He began to ease it out.

And she grabbed. Grabbed at the whole wallet.

But not with quite enough force. His fingers, half-useless though they were most of the time, had tightened hard on the wallet's lower edge.

'No, you don't,' he shouted, feeling the red rage powering up inside his head.

'Shut up, you old fool,' she screamed back.

A harder tug at the thick-crammed wallet. He felt the smooth leather begin to slide from between his clawing nails.

The rage in him was pounding now. The sudden anger that in his first days making Merry Bars had swiftly lost any incompetent employee his job.

He dropped his stick and swung up his other hand to get a double grip.

Then she hit him. Somewhere to the side of his nose.

It was a half-hearted blow, altogether lacking in vigour. But it was enough. A blackness closed down over his eyes. He was just aware that the wallet had gone from between his fingers. He even half-heard the clatter of her heels as she ran off.

He succeeded somehow in staying on his feet, drawing in one harsh, sucking breath upon another. Then, after what seemed just a moment or two of blind staggering, he realised that he had to get back to the flat. Pellet would see to him. Lie him down. Send for a doctor.

He forced himself to set off.

But it was hard to see anything. Where was he? He must have got himself right out into the roadway. Was there traffic coming? He tried to listen.

There seemed to be no early vehicles speeding along the wide, vacant stretch of tarmac. So, despite the pulsing red fog in his eyes, he forced himself once more to move forwards.

Come on, my boy. Used to pride yourself on your energy. Show a bit of spirit now. On you go. One step after another. That's the way. You can do it. Never mind that damned stick. You get about without it indoors, you can manage now.

But, God, it's a long way across. Must be shuffling about like a clapped-out old man.

He gave a little ironic grunt.

Well, that's what you are, you idiot. A clapped-out old man.

But, by God, I'll make it yet. However wide this damn road seems.

Come on now, blink your eyes. Clear your vision. Can't be all that far now.

But what's this? Green? Green?

Grass? It can't be grass. But it is. Grass down by my side.

Oh, Christ. I'm in the bloody Gardens. I'm on the path. I've swung right round somehow. I'm going the wrong way altogether.

Heading towards Physical Energy.

Turn round, and…

No. No, damn it, I'd never make it. Not the way I'm feeling now.

So it's going to be at the foot of Physical Energy after all. Under the horse. My horse. My spring of force. Well, where I wanted most. I think.

But will I get there? Hell of a long way.

Hell of a long way.